THE NIGHT OF BROKEN GLASS

Feroz Rather is currently a doctoral student of Creative Writing at Florida State University and his work has appeared in The *Millions,* The *Rumpus,* The *Southeast Review, Caravan, Warscapes, Berfrois,* and *Himal.* His most recent essay, 'Poet in Srinagar', appeared in the anthology *Mad Heart, Be Brave: On the Poetry of Agha Shahid Ali. The Night of Broken Glass* is his first book.

THE NIGHT OF
BROKEN GLASS

FEROZ RATHER

HarperCollins *Publishers* India

First published in India by
HarperCollins *Publishers* in 2018
A-75, Sector 57, Noida, Uttar Pradesh 201301, India
www.harpercollins.co.in

2 4 6 8 10 9 7 5 3 1

P-ISBN: 978-93-5264-161-1
E-ISBN: 978-93-5264-162-8

Typeset in 11.5/15 Adobe Garamond at
Manipal Digital Systems, Manipal

Printed and bound at
Thomson Press (India) Ltd

To my father, Ismaiel

History didn't greet us with triumphal fanfares:
— It flung dirty sand into our eyes.
Ahead of us lay long roads leading nowhere,
poisoned wells and bitter bread.

Our wartime loot is knowledge of the world.
— Wislawa Szymborska

1
The Old Man in the Cottage

❧

I gazed westward from the top of the hill. The cottage where Inspector Masoodi's son had recently moved his father stood in the thin clearing by the lake. Its old wooden walls painted over in a dark shade of green, the cottage had two narrow slits for the windows in the front. Between them, a door clung to a feeble frame on rusting metal hinges – a door that I could break with a single blow of my axe.

I had come to see the cowherd, Gulzar, who reared my master's cows along with the rest of his herd. He was a thin boy of sixteen with a soft face bursting with a new beard and pimples. Whatever the season, he never took off his long woollen *pheran*. Although he always carried a stout staff, I had rarely seen him hit a cow, and that only when it tore away from the herd to enter someone's kitchen or front garden. He hit his cows below the shoulder – never on the haunches – gently guiding them back. Like me, he was not much of a talker. But while I had lost my loquacity during my time inside the prison, Gulzar was quiet by disposition. As soon as he had his herd settled on the slope, between the foot of the hill – where I had walked down to and was standing now – and the courtyard of the cottage thick with willows – which I kept an eye on – he reclined on the grass. Then, from the deep side-pocket of his pheran, he produced his flute of rosewood.

'This makes me and the cows happy,' he said before he began to play.

In summer, when the air became hot and full of mosquitoes and other blood-sucking insects, Gulzar sweated profusely, giving off an odour. However, I never told him to remove his pheran or ever complained about his lack of hygiene. I could not imagine him as someone capable of beating me and I liked him. His reticence, his raggedness, his sour smell and his unshaven pimply face infused a sense of security and self-worth in me.

I saw Inspector Masoodi's son standing by the wire zareba that fenced the courtyard in. He had his father's cold, expressionless face. His eyes were deep and bloodshot, and filled with contempt as he stared at me rudely. I understood his unspoken command beckoning me to go to him so he could charge me with an errand. He came close to the fence.

'I want you to clear the lawn,' he said peremptorily. He sounded haughty but in need of me.

I looked him straight in the eye, confronting his arrogance for a moment. Then I smiled quickly and said, 'I can bring you an axe from my master's house.' Although his eyes softened a bit, his face remained the same – frigid.

'Where is your master's house?' he asked. I turned around and pointed to the top of the hill. 'I will pay you well if you help me cut the willows,' he said.

'Do not worry about the money,' I replied.

I walked up the hill to my master's house. Everything in the house belonged to him. And, because I had told him that I had no one in the world, he felt that I belonged to him as well. In any case, I was ready to risk his wrath for Masoodi's son. I looked for the axe that I had hidden under the staircase in the corridor a while ago. I found it securely wrapped inside a bundle of dusty gunny bags, just where I had left it. I weighed it in my hands as I picked it up. It was a light axe with a heavy head, perfect for chopping. I touched the metal with my hand and then furtively looked around. When I was completely assured of my master's absence, I licked the edge clean with my tongue. I liked the taste of cold metal on my tongue. I went down the hill and offered Masoodi's son the axe.

Over the sound of his blows on the willow trunks and branches, I heard his father cough. The trunks and branches were gnarly and he was soon exhausted. He panted outside while his father coughed inside. All this panting and coughing seemed strangely ludicrous, both father and son in a state of utter helplessness, and for a moment there, I nearly burst out laughing.

'Can you give him some water?' Masoodi's son asked abruptly. I rose from the ground and obliged mutely.

However, as soon as I was inside the dark cottage, my mirth could no longer be held in check and I laughed out loud in reckless jubilation that he had finally asked for my help. For years I had dreamt of this very moment.

I stood in the kitchen, groping in the sudden darkness after the glare of the sunlight outside. As soon as my eyes adjusted to the gloom, I dipped a tumbler into the copper pitcher on the sink. I noticed a knife gleaming on the shelf above. I did not touch the knife, but the sight of its shiny metal thrilled me. The water was cold and I wondered whether it would have a debilitating effect on Inspector Masoodi's already weakened lungs. They sounded rotten and depleted every time he coughed. Would the cold water trigger a fresh bout of hacking?

When I entered Inspector Masoodi's room, I could not believe the sight that met my eyes. His body had shrunk to less than half its size. He lay on the bed, facing the ceiling, his arms crossed over his chest. His long, oval face was furrowed with wrinkles. His eyes were closed. His mouth was slightly open, and his lips were colourless as though contoured with dry chalk. He moaned like a patient in need of an injection of morphine. When he opened his eyes, he did not look at me. He stretched out his hand, probably thinking that his son had entered the room.

'Water,' he croaked, 'water …'

For a moment, I felt I should retreat. The change in him was so drastic that I wondered how much I may have changed as well. I felt terrible thinking about the past. I was not sure of playing the final part of the game that I had imagined playing when I had seen him last, twenty-five years ago. During every moment of this time, I had rebelled against the idea that he was alive in the very same world in which I also lived. Thinking of what he had done to me and how he had damaged me, my heartbeats sounded like the rattle of gunfire. I looked at him again, incredulous. This was the same man. I wanted to end it all then and there, in a flash. But something held me back. I don't completely understand it. I was not afraid of his son. Perhaps I wanted to see Inspector Masoodi die a slow and painful death.

The tumbler shook as I handed it to him and the water spilled on to his clothes. I gently raised his head. He had lost most of his luxuriant dark hair. The few straggly strands he still retained at the sides and back of his head were grey and unwashed. I took the tumbler from his hand and raised it to his lips. I could hear his son chopping at the willows furiously; the blows of the metal against the flesh of the wood. I did not look into the old man's eyes. He breathed stertorously; each breath was an ascending wave of pain. At the top, as it faltered, I slipped a few droplets of water into his mouth. Inspector Masoodi made a wheezing sound and his shrunken belly billowed. As the water went down, his breath descended sharply, ending like a sad sigh. It was hard to believe that this was the same man I had known so closely at the beginning of the war; this pathetic creature who was nothing but a few ounces of flabby flesh clinging to a brittle bone-cage. I looked at him, at his broken skin and the weak hands that had once struck me with fury and violence.

How close to death you are, Inspector Masoodi, I thought. I gnashed my teeth and outside his son continued to wield the axe on the hapless willows.

When I emerged from the cottage, I saw Masoodi's son almost hidden in the tall grass as he lay beside a tall pile of chopped willow branches. He had the same lean body and broad shoulders that his father once had. But, looking at him lying in the grass, I wondered what kind of shroud the grass would make if it were used to cover his corpse. I was not convinced that the thought was worth the consideration. Inspector Masoodi's pallor was in my eyes. I sensed the slow arrival of his death that would gradually eat away what was left of his flesh and bones. When his son rose, I jerked my head towards the house and asked him what the problem was.

'Lung cancer,' he replied. 'Terminal stage.' The sweat was dripping off his brow and he had a small wound on his left forearm that had bled for a while. He had wiped the blood with his right hand which was still stained red. I decided that the expressionlessness of his face came from his father and I hated it. However, what I did like was that he was unsentimental about his father's condition. Some time ago, I had met Gulzar as he was making his way down the hill. We stopped to chat and he told me that this man was a police officer as well. I reckoned that because his father fell ill long before he was sixty, the retirement age in the police force, the son had the opportunity and compulsion to step into his father's shoes. The young man had been none too pleased about it because he had wanted to become a civil officer, a bureaucrat. In a place like ours, where the war was slow, subtle and camouflaged, becoming a civil officer gave one immense power, although most of these officers came across as benign and harmless. Gulzar also told me that the son lived with his wife and her parents in the city. He did not like living with Inspector Masoodi. The sight of the dying old man distressed his wife and his in-laws, so the son had shifted the father to the cottage for his final days.

'Will you look after the old man while I am away?' he asked now.

'When will you come back?'

'After two days, on Sunday.'

The only way that he could have had any inkling about my true identity would have been by interrogating Gulzar who delivered a bottle of fresh milk at the cottage every evening. Twenty-five years ago, in the dead of night, Inspector Masoodi and his friend, Major S, had tossed my half-dead body, tied to a huge rock, into the lake. My file had been closed by the high command because they assumed I was dead like the innumerable prisoners whom I had met and befriended in the prison and whose bodies, pale in the moonlight, I saw at the bottom of the lake.

I looked into his eyes. Upon seeing no signs of suspicion there, I smiled and said: 'Yes, sir.'

A thick willow branch, overhanging the roof, threatened to block the doorway. I told him that it was too high for me to chop it down. He rolled his eyes in contempt and strode into the cottage, emerging a few minutes later with an old chair. He placed the chair in front of the door. 'There,' he gritted angrily.

I climbed onto the chair, the axe in my right hand and my left hand on his shoulder. I could see that he parted his hair in the centre like his father. I could see his bare scalp at the parting. How would it sound, the axe smashing into his skull? What a delightful cracking sound it would make. I swung at the branch with such force that the axe rebounded from the roof, fell from my hands and landed at the policeman's feet.

As he knelt to pick it up from the ground, the branch broke and fell, crashing down on the man's wounded forearm.

I jumped down from the chair as he tamped down on his agony. I moved the branch away and examined his arm. I took the axe back from him and watched a drop of blood welling up as the wound began to bleed afresh. In any case, he was not the kind of man who would know how to use an axe. His casual cotton chinos and linen shirt suggested urbanity and a refinement of style. It unnerved me, however, how coldly unsentimental he was. He did not groan or even wince. Like his father in his youth, he gave an impression of toughness and brutal control. When he spoke, the words fell from his lips like hard slabs of granite.

'My father has taught me how to use a gun and I can do that well,' he said. 'But you need to learn to wield your axe wisely.'

I nodded at him, again looking him in the eye. Inside, Inspector Masoodi coughed and mumbled something that we could not understand. His son did not budge. He continued to pinion me with a piercing stare that would have terrified any other man. However, I had already looked death in the eye, so I stared back unflinchingly. I saw the muscles of his face tauten for an instant before he allowed himself to relax into a cold smile. He needed me. He patted my shoulder and asked me whether I could check on his father. I went inside and gave the old man another glass of water.

When I came out, the son was not to be seen. I quickly made my way to the willow stumps. An axe-toting shadow loomed up from behind me. I whirled around to find him standing close behind me. He handed me the axe.

'There are packets of soup in the kitchen,' he said.

'I do not need them,' I said.

'My father will. If there is an emergency, call me. The phone is in the corridor.' He scribbled a number on a slip of paper and thrust it into my shirt pocket.

ॐ

The willows had laid a siege to the cottage from all sides. They were of the genus which grew profusely in the higher Himalayas and in the forlorn villages of Ladakh. They proliferated with multitudinous shoots and created thick, impenetrable tangles. Neither the lake nor the city beyond were visible through Inspector Masoodi's bedroom window. The last rays of the setting sun died in the tumorous growth that blocked my view.

As night fell, beastly noises emanated from the undergrowth almost as if some wild animal had descended from the hill and had entered the coppice with the aim of devouring a moorhen sleeping in its nest. I sat by the bed, close to Inspector Masoodi's head. His bib had flecks of blood and the thick mucus that he coughed up. When I touched him on the shoulder, he shuddered so violently that I thought he was going to collapse. I poured water into his mouth. As the water went down his gullet, it somehow calmed him. I raised his head and slipped two soft pillows beneath it. I dithered for a while wondering how to pacify him and alleviate the pain. I stirred the contents of the bowl on the bedside table and then raised the spoon to his mouth. His hairy nostrils quivered as he inhaled the hot vapours. His mouth opened like the that of a frog and he stuck his tongue out delicately lapping up the soup with the tip of his tongue. This seemed to warm him up a bit and he rallied a little. My conversation with him was a one-sided monologue because, as his son had mentioned, Inspector Masoodi could barely speak.

When he was done having a spoonful – and that was all he could eat – I went to the other bedroom. The walls were rotting and porous with large cracks in the ceiling beams. Spiders dangled from the cobwebs in the corners. I went outside and returned with the axe. I put it under the bed that I planned to sleep in. Inspector Masoodi had another coughing fit. I could hear the fatal beckoning of the hacking against the deepening sounds of the night insects outside. However, I was exhausted. I sprawled out on the bed, folding my arms under my head. Inspector Masoodi was probably dozing now. It became difficult to sleep. Here he was on the verge of death. The same man who had captured me and handed me to Major S. Would he ever know the pain of being sold by a fellow countryman to an outsider? What kind of shackles were these which withheld me from hacking his body to pieces?

Major S had suspended me by my feet in the prison cell where I had been incarcerated. I was stripped naked and my hands were tied behind my back with coarse rope. Inspector Masoodi was the only person who knew that I had attacked Major S a month ago. In an attempt to prevent the army's invasion, I had lobbed a grenade at the major's cavalcade. The grenade had detonated a few metres from the bonnet of his jeep, the shrapnel smashing the windshield. Major S had been mildly injured by the shards of flying glass. What had enraged him even more was the realization that to tackle me he was wholly dependent on the goodwill of the local police officer.

In retaliation, Major S whipped me viciously with his belt until my limbs swelled and my skin turned red and blue.

I screamed in agony. Such was the magnitude of my pain that I felt the city was crying with me. The lake swelled, and the hills shattered to mounds of ash. I did not lose consciousness. I felt my pain. I was responsible for what I had done; I was conscious of the cause that drove me to violence and kindled the desire for justice in my heart. My path was a long dark tunnel where the rocks exploded and tore open the walls to splatter blood onto my feet. At the end of the tunnel, as I marched forth, I saw the light of freedom, *aazadi*.

The iron-cage in which I was manacled rattled. I saw Inspector Masoodi enter. He was in his khakhi police uniform, apparently different from Major S's dark, olive-green regimentals. He had a baton in his hand with which he proceeded to hit me, making the bruises bleed. I wailed and he hit me harder. Major S stood by spurring him on.

'Is this what you smoke?' he asked, extracting the pack of Revolution from my trouser pocket. He took one out and lit it. As he took a drag, he coughed. The peculiar scent of the smoke that was fragrant to me irritated his eyes. He asked Inspector Masoodi to back away. He obligingly moved out of the cage and took a ringside seat on a chair by the door.

'Masoodi, now enjoy the show,' Major S said, coughing, his eyes watering.

I knew what he was going to do: burn me with the tip of the Revolution. The part of my body that he chose to torture was my buttock.

As I screamed in humiliation and pain, Major S laughed, searing a circle around my anus.

'Nasty, nasty, nasty,' he said, chortling and pointing his stubby finger at my anus. He took a long drag and blew the smoke towards my anus. 'There goes the smoke of Revolution.'

Inspector Masoodi was silent and Major S glanced at him suspiciously. He wondered whether he had somehow crossed a line with his crassness and whether he had lost an ally who felt bound to shift loyalties to the other side – my side.

'*Rate tschute aazadi*. Arse, take in freedom,' Inspector Masoodi said softly in Kashmiri, corroborating Major S.

After a pause, Major S laughed and Inspector Masoodi laughed and laughed so hard that tears welled in his eyes too and he almost fell out of the chair in merriment.

Inspector Masoodi! Inspector Masoodi! What was I supposed to do with this Inspector Masoodi now that it was cancer and not me killing him?

After surviving the torments of prison and the murderous depths of the lake, after years of living away from my city I masqueraded as a shawl-seller in Ladakh for a while. During this time I had spent every waking moment planning my revenge while adopting such a subservient and resigned manner that I blended into any background. I had come back to this village as a domestic servant and found a job near the cottage. I had befriended Gulzar and had manipulated him to spy for me and give me information about Inspector Masoodi's movements. He had told me that until a few years ago, Inspector Masoodi came every Sunday night to this secluded cottage to drink with his friends. Later, I nearly fainted with joy when he told me that I did not need to cross the lake and scour the city looking for him because his own son was going to bring him here. This was a stroke of luck.

I was agitated. I went into the dark kitchen and struck a match to light a candle. The knife gleamed in the firelight.

In Inspector Masoodi's bedroom, I put the candle on the bedside table and sat on the chair by the dying man's bedside. He was still breathing. But it was so faint and rasping that I could barely hear life within him. I was torn now. I wanted to put the knife to his throat and slit it open, but then he was seized by a paroxysm of coughing and was thrown out of his doze. I put the knife on the table beside the candle to grab a fresh towel from the wardrobe, aware that he would spit out blood in a few minutes.

He wheezed, gasping for breath. His eyes bulged out. 'Water, water,' he begged.

I made him sip and as the water went down his gullet he threw up. His entire body was convulsing as he coughed again, spitting out blobs of blood and mucus. I held him firmly, but the force of the convulsions did not abate. I wiped the blobs from around his mouth and chest. I held his head tight in my hands. Then, suddenly, the fit passed. He was so exhausted that he immediately fell asleep.

I returned to my room. It was very late. I lay in bed and closed my eyes. My thoughts whirled in my head as I pictured Gulzar telling Inspector Masoodi's son that I had enquired about him and his father. I felt that this was all an elaborate trap into which I had fallen so easily. He was going to come for me while I was asleep and shoot me dead. I was suddenly very afraid. My head felt hot and feverish and I had to suppress this idea hard to fall asleep.

When I woke up, I opened the window. The day was dawning and the sunlight spread through the willows like a distant, doleful sensation.

I returned to Inspector Masoodi. I did not look at his face, but I touched his shoulder. It was cold and frigid. I knew he was dead. I was tempted to look at his face, but I did not. It was I who was in power now; I was almost sure that if I looked at him, I would mutilate him. I knew his mouth must be open, as would his eyes. I did not make any effort to shut them. I picked up the knife from the side table and put it back in the kitchen.

I took the chit out of my pocket and called his son. 'Your father is dead,' I said.

He sighed but said nothing. He was lying by the side of his wife whose breath I heard rising and falling serenely in the background. Had he wept or shown any emotion, I would have told him who I was. I would have told him that had his father been healthy, I would have chopped his body up and thrown him into the lake. It was obvious that his father's death had brought him relief. He would share the news with his wife as soon as she woke up.

I did not know where to direct my anger. I was furious and frustrated. I found myself holding on to the telephone long after he had hung up. Tears gathered in my eyes. In a sudden frenzy I yanked at the telephone wire. I pulled so hard that I hurt my hand. The receiver fell to the floor. I kicked it hard and it smashed to smithereens against the wall. I punched the rotting wall with my hand and broke a plank. Through the gap, I had one final glimpse of Inspector Masoodi.

I went into the bedroom where I had spent the night, picked up my axe and walked out of the cottage.

2
The Pheran

❧

1

It was the month of November, damp and bleak. But that afternoon the sky filled with brilliant light pouring blue into the horizons where clouds lay like mountains of tousled snow. The old, three-storeyed house stood by the main road that ran through central Srinagar, parallel to the river Jhelum.

As Wali was away at work, Maryam sat close to Safir in a wicker chair in the back garden, their knees touching. He leaned towards her and brushed back a tendril of her hair that had worked loose, whispering something to her that sounded like a dirty joke. Maryam had only heard the words 'tickle' and 'butt-crack', but that was enough for her to throw back her head and send the garden resounding with her laughter. She moved in closer to her boyfriend and was about to place her ear close to his lips again when she sensed Wali looming in the kitchen door behind her.

As her father stepped into the garden, Safir stood up immediately, sheepishly greeting him.

'Sit, sit,' said Wali coldly as Maryam disappeared into the house.

As he subsided back into the cane chair, Wali remained standing before him.

'What's your name?' he asked.

'Safir.'

Maryam had mentioned his name many times during their conversations.

'Where are you from?' Wali asked.

'I am from here … from Srinagar,' Safir replied.

'And what do you do?' Wali asked.

'I write,' said Safir after a moment's hesitation.

'That's fine, but what do you do?'

'I write,' repeated Safir.

'Writing, etc., is fine,' the short, wizened old man stepped closer, 'but what exactly do you do?' He took off his thick-rimmed spectacles and his myopic eyes went blank. As Safir raised his eyes to meet them, an awkward silence fell between them.

Safir glanced at the time on his cell phone, 'I should go,' he said, rising.

'Have tea with us,' Wali said, slipping his glasses back on. He beckoned Maryam, who was watching them anxiously through the kitchen window, and asked her to bring out the tea.

'Papa, give me a few minutes,' she called back, turning off the faucet that she'd turned on to wash the cups that were already clean.

'Thank you, sir, but some other time,' Safir said and walked away from Wali.

When he entered the kitchen, he was sweating. 'I'll go now,' he muttered, without looking at Maryam and made a dash for the front door.

Maryam did not want to talk to her father as they sat in the sitting room for dinner that evening. However, winter was around the corner and she had to tell him that they needed to stock up: spices, rice, cooking oil, pulses and dried vegetables. Wali knew that all this would entail a lot of expenditure, but sensing he had upset his daughter, he readily assented.

With Maryam busy preparing for her college exams, the rest of the month flew by, with extremely short periods of daylight. At the beginning of December, on the day that Wali retired as the head clerk from Jammu and Kashmir Bank, it snowed and he fell ill. The doctors advised Maryam to avoid giving him spicy or oily food. His lungs were weak and his throat, parched and dry. He needed to be kept warm with extra blankets and duvets in a warm room. Maryam planted him on a bed with two mattresses in the sitting room by the kitchen and wrapped him in two blankets and a thick woollen quilt. She put fresh pillows under his head and placed a spittoon by the bed.

When her mother had abandoned her father, sixteen years ago, she had been only eight years old. She missed her mother and had tried to fill the void by imposing her authority in all the three storeys of the house. She grew to enjoy being in charge of the household without having to answer to anyone. She had managed to run the house, efficiently stretching Wali's thin salary to make ends meet and then later supplemented his income by embroidering pherans. In her room on the third storey, she would rise early and spend the mornings making venations of leaves – elm, almond, walnut, cherry and willow – around the necklines, down the fronts and around hemlines and borders of the sleeves of the pherans. She had often resented schoolwork and textbooks, and her routine household chores, and it was here, in the privacy of her room, pricking the cloth, that she released that anger. With each delicate stitch, she wondered whether she could develop a script to instruct her future children with Safir in the intricate art of embroidery; she wondered whether she could begin their lessons even as she suckled them at her breasts, abrading their soft cheeks against the hard threads of silver.

As soon as the temperature rose from -5°c to 15°c and the snow disappeared, Wali's condition improved. He asked Maryam to put away the mattresses and blankets. Instead of Corex – the sickly sweet cough syrup that burnt the lining of his stomach and made his head heavy – he asked her to buy him a potion from Kozghar's and half a dozen apple saplings from the market.

Maryam boarded a mini-bus which took her over Zero Bridge to the Cantonment with a bunker at the beginning of the front fence of corrugated tin sheets. Over the fence, she saw the sprawling concrete multi-storeyed building where the soldiers camped, and behind the building was the Wall soaring into the sky. The road gently arced along the western shore of the lake and finally reached Kashmir University.

She caught up with Safir and they skived classes and went to Lofty Chinars. They sat side by side on the shore of the lake under a huge sycamore tree. Safir lit up a Revolution for her which she smoked as she contemplated the oval lake tapering towards the city. Along the soft curves of the lake's shores, looking at the still green water, the branches of the willows hung low. She heard the calls of lapwings and moorhens. From behind the lines of boat houses emerged boats loaded with flowers from stern to stern. Because she was looking at the city from the distance she deliberately sought, her heart filled with a sudden and sharp longing to return.

Across the lake, she glimpsed the top of a hill. Rumour had it that the soldiers in the Cantonment planned to dig into the hill for the raw material to extend the Wall into the city. They were going to employ two yellow bulldozers to raze the market town at the foot of the hill. When she had first heard about this dreadful plan, she had pictured bulldozers lumbering up the steep slopes, the gleaming teeth of their buckets remorselessly piercing the green soil. As these monstrous machines crested the hill, they would leave behind a city in ruins below with bodies crushed under the debris. For many nights, just before going to sleep, she had imagined that upon her arrival on the scene on a quiet noon, she would be all alone. She would run from one mound of rubble to another, and unable to pull out the corpses by their hands, visible and outstretched, she would become tired and frustrated. She would stop trying and stand straight, terrified by the sight of her own blood-splattered hands illumined by the blazing sun.

She was grateful for the foliage of the willow trees that obstructed her view of the base of the hill and the doomed market town. She rested her head on Safir's shoulder and sighed contentedly, asking for another Revolution.

As she puffed at the cigarette, she reached for and clutched Safir's hand. A haze of smoke spread over her head and wafted towards the lake.

༃

Wali was bent double as he dug up the earth by the dilapidated poplar picket fence in his backyard. Lumps of loosened soil lay at his feet and, as the dusk approached, he planted the last of his six new saplings in a winding row.

'Dear Papa,' Maryam thought affectionately, glimpsing him through the kitchen window. 'For years you slaved away in Jammu and Kashmir Bank and even now you have not ceased your toil.'

As she took out the flagon of rose sherbet from the refrigerator, she thought back to the day when Wali had evicted Safir from their house. Once Safir left, her father had come inside the house to wash his face and arms in the bathroom. He had gone back to the garden quickly to pray on the faded, dwindling grass. Despite the glow of peace on his forehead and the posture that suggested nothing but calmness and repose, Maryam had wanted to scream at him and tell him that Mama was right in leaving him for another man. Wali, with his clumsiness and bad habit of intruding, didn't quite measure up to match Mama's beauty as that other man did. However, Maryam was aware that Mama had been very cruel to Papa. She had left him for the bank manager who was Wali's boss at the time, and only a few days after Wali had hosted a dinner for the man. Wali, who had hoped that the gesture would win him a promotion, lost his wife instead. He had vowed not to remarry and devoted himself to the care of his daughter with a quiet ferocity. He had spent money on Maryam's clothes, shoes, books and notebooks.

Maryam poured out a glass of chilled sherbet for her Papa and tasted it. She giggled as she suddenly remembered how Safir had exited like a scalded cat that day, his macho self-image in tatters.

She looked at her father again, at his forehead glistening with sweat. She grabbed another glass from the shelf and poured herself a drink as well and went outside. He threw the shovel to a side, straightened his back and smiled.

'When did you come back from the university?' he asked by way of greeting. He was panting a little after his exertions in the garden.

'I made this for you in the morning before I left,' she said, ignoring his question, and smiling affectionately as he drank thirstily.

'Is there more?' he asked.

'Yes, Papa. Would you like some more?'

'Yes, please,' he replied.

When she returned with another tall frosted glass, he was seated in a patio chair surveying his saplings intently. As she walked towards him, without turning and facing her he said, 'I've not seen Safir for a while now,' he said.

'He must be busy, Papa. He reports for the *Informer* now.'

'Do they pay him well?'

'Yes, they do,' she said, shortly.

'Wise boy! I knew he'd get the point.'

Maryam frowned and looked away. Her father was old; his sparse grey hair could no longer hide his cracked and discoloured scalp; his wrinkles were deep grooves; his body was stooped and flabby. It was the natural erosion of age, gradually shrivelling and withering the human body. How could Wali, so obviously in the fading twilight of his life, understand what Safir inspired in Maryam?

Wali's feet, shod in Liberty leather shoes with worn soles, dangled several inches above the ground as he perched on the chair. He had to stretch his short legs to alight. He was still out of breath. He slurped the sherbet noisily, the liquid dribbling from the corners his mouth and trickling down to the cleft of his unshaven chin.

The cold drink seemed to pacify him. His breathing calmed down and his perspiration disappeared. He carelessly dropped the glass tumbler by his feet and sat back to survey the row of newly planted saplings, the picket fence and the silent backs of the houses beyond.

Maryam put her hands on his shoulders, gently massaging them. She wondered whether he was even aware of her presence as he contemplated the cracks in the wood, the flakes of peeling white paint sticking to each picket. He had been planning to work on this for months.

ॐ

Wali had wanted Maryam to write the aptitude test that would qualify her to become a junior clerk in the Jammu and Kashmir Bank. He had even offered to bring home the new manager, who had the final say in the selection, and host a dinner for him. However, Maryam had her own plans for her future. At the end of the that year, when she completed her MA in journalism from Kashmir University, she joined the *Informer*.

For her first story, she walked away from the *Informer* offices to Badshah Bridge and went to the Kozghar's. Inside the shop hung a faint aroma of rose petals and mould. The owner, a middle-aged man of Turkish descent with a dense, black beard and deep, pensive eyes that seemed to glitter with the peril of extinction, who lived in semi-darkness surrounded by empty, cracked and dusty glass jars on wooden shelves, emerged from the rear of the shop.

'What can I do for you?' he said as a greeting.

'I want to buy some sherbet,' she said.

'Yes, of course. Please come in and sit down.' When they were seated in the dingy room, she told him that she wished to write about him.

'I am the master of a dying trade,' the man said sadly. His family had been living in the city for the last 400 years and he feared that he was the last in their line of trade. With the advent of modern medicine, his sales had plummeted and the practice of making sherbets, lucrative once, was on the verge of dying out completely. The only thing that sustained the shop was the sale of rosewater to the mosques, where it was sprinkled on the walls on Fridays.

'I am happy to write about you,' Maryam said. 'I also want to buy a jar of rosewater and another one extracted from starflower.'

'Do you mean *Kahzabaan*?' he asked.

'Kahzabaan,' Maryam nodded vigorously, repeating the native name after him. The Kozghar disappeared into the dark recesses of his shop to reappear with some jars that he put on the counter.

'If you can convince the city to somehow save my tottering business,' he said, 'I'll give you these for free.'

Maryam chuckled at that. She knew she would not take anything from the old man without paying for it. She threatened to leave the jars behind and walk away when he waved away her money.

'Oh, alright, I'll take the money,' he grumbled, 'but please allow me to give you this.'

'What is *this*?' Maryam asked curiously when he produced a vial of mysterious purplish liquid.

'This is called *araq neelofar*,' he said. 'This herbal medicine is good for the kidneys and purifies the blood. And perhaps the last bottle I made.'

ॐ

'Your English is good,' the boss remarked, glancing through her article. 'However, your feature is more like a character sketch in a novella than a work of journalism.'

She was not sure whether this was sincere constructive criticism but continued writing short reports and long features. She explored various parts of the city, talking to the womenfolk, both young and old. When she returned home in the evenings, she barely had any energy to cook or embroider a pheran. The persistent clatter of the office keyboards that still rung in her brain drowned out the calls of moorhens and lapwings.

Months passed and she slipped into the mechanical routine of the editorial office. According to her boss, her articles had improved immensely – they were now succinct, crisp and impersonal.

In the beginning, when she had started working, she had felt a strange detachment within herself. This curious feeling akin to emptiness and boredom persisted and she realized that she could no longer appreciate simple things like the beauty of nature or enjoy the taste of food. Using the elevator at work upset her system and made her nauseous, causing her stomach to convulse. Her head ached dully.

One Saturday, she woke up early and cooked an elaborate lunch for Papa and herself. After lunch, she picked up an envelope, walked to Zero Bridge, descended the narrow staircase and made her way to the riverbank.

She desperately hoped that Safir wouldn't be in the office. She reached the huge, three-storeyed building with the posh marble floor and elevator. She hesitantly pressed the button to go up to the third storey.

As soon as she stepped out of the elevator, she saw her boss and Safir through the open door. They were sitting in the common area, discussing new story ideas over cigarettes and strong tea.

Maryam silently put her envelope on the table before them.

'What's this?' her boss asked.

'I'm resigning,' she replied.

'Why?' asked Safir.

'That is none of your business, Safir,' she snapped and walked out of the office.

Safir felt hurt that Maryam snubbed him in front of their boss. The boss tore the envelope and began reading the letter. He was flitting his eyes from one side to the other.

'This girl lives in cuckoo-land,' he said derogatorily. He was so enraged, he disregarded the *Informer's* protocol; instead of placing the letter in Maryam's personal folder, he crumpled it in his palm and tossed it into the trash bin. 'I want you to have your story ready in two hours. We can do without her bullshit,' he said to Safir and stormed out.

Safir fished out the letter from the trash bin and went into his cubicle, closing the door behind him. His hands were trembling slightly as he steeled himself to read Maryam's letter:

Dear Sir,

 While I was in college, I realized that my father was growing old. I began to worry about my future and I taught myself to do embroidery work. In my aunt's house, on the southern shore of the lake, I sat for hours on end with a bunch of girls, poor girls, who could not afford school, with lovely pherans spread across their laps. They worked diligently with sharp needles which sometimes pricked their fingertips, drawing blood. Nevertheless, they persevered; they stitched and embroidered. I too sat with them and learnt their craft. And it took me hours to create my first almond leaf and several hours of patient application to bestow its venations.

My days at the *Informer*, listening to the empty prattle and clatter, have been deeply disturbing. There is no silence here. And the practice of journalism, brave and risky without doubt, also means being visible, vain and close to power. If I continue here, I am in danger of losing touch with stitching and my ability to reflect and contemplate.

I don't know whether juxtaposing journalism with stitching is justified. But I do know that working with a needle in silence created possibilities of humility and surrender for me. That is not the case with journalism. If I were a man like you and Safir, I too might follow the ways that seem necessary to our practice. I too might cultivate buddies in the police, call an Inspector Masoodi to Cafe Barbarica for a drink. And in the moments I gossip with him, I will grow loud and I will start guffawing; I will have a false sense of power, a caged dog's chance to jump and bark and bite vengefully at my own while I am still on a leash. I will forget how blood, still hot and roaring on the streets I walk, is slowly seeping into the soul of our city. I will forget the nightmares of destruction that I plunge into every time I sleep. This sense of entitlement is duplicitous; this duplicity fills me with revulsion and discomfort.

I say no to the *Informer*. Thank you.

Yours,
Maryam

ॐ

That evening, Maryam got a call from Safir. Upon knowing that she was feeling upset and had gone to Jabin Aunty's, he offered to bring her home. That was sweet of him, she thought, but she told him she would manage.

She could hear their boss grunting at Safir in the background, so she advised him to hang up. At that instant, a sudden power cut left her standing in the dark in a long corridor. She wondered whether this was a sign from God about the rightness or wrongness of her decision to quit her job without notice. She slipped her mobile phone into the side pocket of her dress and walked into the kitchen where Jabin was lighting a lamp on the windowsill. Her aunt turned around, smiling.

'I won't let you go without having dinner with us,' she said.

'The Cantonment soldiers make me nervous,' Maryam protested, 'and I don't want to go home after dark in an autorickshaw.'

'It has been months since I last saw you,' Jabin said. 'I'll ask Ishfaq to give you a ride home.'

Maryam could not refuse. She went into the dark corridor again and stood leaning against the wall. The darkness brought back her feelings of ambivalence. She wondered whether she had acted recklessly by being too idealistic. In any case, the thought that she would now have more time for her favourite activity, embroidering, made her happy. She pressed the buttons of her tiny, silver-coloured mobile phone and its screen glowed.

The landline telephone at her home still had the signature style ringtone of the nineteenth century and rang several times until her father finally answered her call. He had dozed off in a chair in the garden, he said apologetically. She knew that she would have to eventually explain her abrupt resignation to him but not now, not over the telephone. Although he would be disappointed, he would not hold it against her and would accept her decision philosophically. She softened her tone as she told him she would be having dinner at her aunt's home.

When she hung up, the entrance door in the front opened. Ishfaq and Iqbal walked in together and smilingly escorted her into the kitchen.

Maryam sat beside Iqbal on the black woollen carpet with a pattern of green circles covering the floor. They both faced the oven where Jabin presided with a ladle in her hand.

Maryam and Iqbal were of the same age while Ishfaq was four years their junior. He sat close to his mother, with his back to brother and cousin, as he talked to his mother about his day.

'How are you Ishfaq?' Maryam interrupted.

'Very well,' he said, without turning around.

'Jabin Aunty tells me you bought a new car today?' He turned briefly to nod and resumed his conversation with his mother. Iqbal whispered something in Maryam's ear.

'Did you buy the green apricots as well?' she asked. Iqbal and Maryam laughed. So did Jabin.

One winter, when Ishfaq was a little child, he had thrown a huge tantrum in the kitchen. The snow had levelled up to the windows, jamming the doors shut, while he sulked and demanded that his father, Mohiddin, brought him green apricots from the market.

'Don't you guys have anything better to do?' growled Ishfaq.

Maryam, sticking her tongue out at him, rose and went up to Jabin.

'Are you done?' she asked her aunt. 'Where is the *dasterkhwan*?'

'The new one is behind the copper cauldron on the top shelf,' Jabin said. 'Can you get that one?' Maryam realized that despite her five feet and five inches, she would not be able to reach the shelf.

'Can you help me?' she asked her cousins. Ishfaq immediately rose. He was as tall as Iqbal with fine features and a chiselled face. He wrapped his arm around the cauldron and moved it aside before rising on his toes to pull the dasterkhwan down.

'What else can I do for you?' he asked sarcastically, placing the tapestry in her hands.

'This will do for now,' she said, teasing her lips into a smile. His foot brushed against hers lightly and their eyes met. At that moment, the door opened and Mohiddin entered the kitchen.

Maryam, whose scarf had slipped on to her shoulders, quickly wrapped it around her head. And assuming a solemn expression, she greeted her uncle.

'I've been caught up with the matters of the mosque,' Mohiddin said, leaning back into a cushion by the wall. 'Otherwise I would have come to visit your father. Is he still at the bank? I went in yesterday, but he wasn't there.'

'He's retired now. He had a bad cold and cough over the winter, but he is feeling much better these days,' she said, spreading the dasterkhwan in front of Mohiddin. Ishfaq and Iqbal sitting on either side of their father twitched the dasterkhwan's ends into place. She gave the men a bowl of water to wash their hands while Jabin ladled the white rice onto the plates and the chicken cooked with spinach and garlic into little copper bowls.

Before they started their meal, Mohiddin turned on the battery-powered radio and surfed through the frequencies until he found Radio Kashmir. Raj Begum was singing a sad song in her melodiously husky voice:

> *rum gayem sheeshas, begour gova bane meoun …*
> My glass cracked, my vessel clanged on …

They all ate together, talking softly. When the song ended, Mohiddin reduced the volume.

'I am as old as your father. I have worked for thirty-eight years at the shop and managed the treasury of the mosque for the past eleven years. I am ready to retire too although, unlike Wali Saheb, I don't have a policy pension.' His sons looked concerned, worried and a little embarrassed by the timing and tone of this remark. They exchanged glances and then looked at Maryam, their eyes telling her that they only half-agreed with what their father had said and that they were sorry if he had embarrassed her. And then, as though burdened with the weight of the implications of that statement, the onus of the household expenditure, their expressions became tense. They lowered their eyes and returned to eating.

'I agree that you should stay at home and put up your feet,' Maryam replied. Mohiddin's eyes twinkled happily. The brothers raised their heads and smiled at Maryam while Aunt Jabin said half-jokingly, 'We are expired now: it's high time we get a daughter-in-law or a couple of daughters-in-law who'll cook and clean, while we old folks relax and listen to Raj Begum.'

Everyone laughed and Maryam was pleased that her presence enlivened this little family. She seemed to fill the void of a daughter in the household. At the same time, she felt apprehensive. Was Jabin Aunty alluding to her when she mentioned daughters-in-law? As soon as they finished eating, she helped her aunt with the dishes and rolled up the dasterkhwan. She sat down with the family once again, handing them toothpicks and candied fennel, until it was time to go, and everyone came to the porch to see her off.

She climbed into the brand new Maruti car parked in the street outside. The seats were still covered in polythene and the windshield was spotless.

The verandas of the new concrete houses encroached into the narrow, potholed road. The tarmac was broken and littered with the garbage that housewives negligently threw out of their kitchen windows. The state of the street saddened and infuriated Maryam as Ishfaq carefully cruised from the foot of the hill towards the city centre. A full moon was rising into the dark sky prickled with the glitter of stars.

'You've always wanted to buy a car since you were very little,' she said.

'Yes,' he replied.

'I like the Maruti,' Maryam said.

'You know nothing about cars,' Ishfaq scoffed. 'This is a new model launched by the company.'

'Then it won't last long,' Maryam retorted.

'How do you mean?' Ishfaq frowned, darting a quick glance at her. She paused, hearing the irritation in his voice. She liked provoking him. She missed Safir. She was feeling bad for having snubbed him.

'Where did you get the money?' she asked Ishfaq.

He did not take his eyes off the road and accelerated as he replied, 'Abba talks about retiring and staying at home. As a matter of fact, he can't live a day away from his shop. He gave me some money and Iqbal gave me some. The rest I put in having saved over the last three years driving passengers in my autorickshaw.'

She was not listening but looking at him. She had a sudden desire to kiss him. She patted his shoulder caressingly. Ishfaq looked at her and finally his lips twitched into a smile. He switched on the stereo fitted in the middle of the dashboard. A Lata Mangeshkar song came on. Maryam grimaced.

'Saccharine and high-pitched,' she said. 'Raj Begum wins every time.'

'Who is Raj Begum?' Ishfaq said.

'Oh, shut up,' Maryam punched his shoulder.

Ishfaq turned off the stereo and began to hum a Raj Begum song.

'No, that does not make you Raj Begum,' Maryam laughed. They were nearing the Cantonment and the moon disappeared behind the Wall.

'Should we avoid Zero Bridge?' Ishfaq asked. 'The soldiers often stop me at night when I pass by in my autorickshaw.'

Maryam agreed. Ishfaq turned right at the roundabout before the Cantonment and went westward on the road by the offices of the *Informer* leading to Badshah Bridge. Then he took a detour and came back on to the road parallel to the river Jhelum.

Wali was squatting at the front door with a lantern in his hand, waiting for his daughter. When he saw the car, he stood up.

Ishfaq greeted him and courteously opened the passenger door for Maryam to disembark.

'Where are you going?' Wali asked Ishfaq. 'Come in. It is too late for you to go home now. You should stay.'

'No, I'll be fine,' he said.

'Stay,' Maryam said. 'Stay the night and you'll go in the morning.'

But Ishfaq shook his head and started the car. He deftly manoeuvred the car around before switching on the stereo. Avoiding the long detour, he drove over Zero Bridge. At the end of the bridge, he heard an ominous clang and the car abruptly stopped right in front of the bunker.

'Motherfucker, move on!' a voice screamed from inside.

Ishfaq was frightened. He turned the key and pushed against the clutch desperately, but the car refused to budge.

'I'm moving … just give me a second, okay,' he cried.

He pressed the clutch again and turned the key in the ignition, but the car did not start. He pushed open the door and quickly moved towards the bonnet to check the engine.

The soldier fired, the bullet ripped through Ishfaq's forehead. He fell face forward onto the bonnet. The soldier fired on, screaming. The blood gurgled out of the holes in Ishfaq's stomach. The semi-digested chicken and spinach spurted out. Bullets shattered the windshield and shards of glass flew over the wooden railing of the bridge and fell into the river.

ॐ

The boss was a stocky man with thickset shoulders and a broad torso. He had a foul tongue and the cunning of a survivor. He got invited to all the parties thrown by Inspector Masoodi. He enjoyed drinking and had cultivated the habit

well; alcohol only heightened his sobriety. From the centre
of his being, he surreptitiously monitored all the people
who moved within his domain. He registered every single
movement and weighed each whisper. Although he did not
give an impression of overt belligerence, he talked with such
an admixture of sweetness and authority that the person
in conversation felt both valued and threatened. In the
common area, he was often surrounded by young reporters
who held him in admiration and awe. They showered him
with compliments, hoping he might by chance open up and
divulge the secret of his success. But the boss talked casually,
revealing nothing. He performed, steadfastly guarding the
enigma of his personality. In the middle of the conversation,
he singled out a reporter. He stared him directly in the
eyes; and for no apparent reason scolding him, halted the
conversation.

After a long moment of tense silence had elapsed, he
clapped. The reporter, harassed and confused, smiled
awkwardly. The boss threw up his arms, clapping harder and
laughing condescendingly.

The boss's performance was reminiscent of the tantrums
of the spoilt, sadistic princes always attended to by big
batches of servants; the princes who had to shout hard at the
servants to deal with the bitterness and alienation because
before the brutal, medieval despots who were their fathers,
they knew they were as utterly useless as they were powerless.

A few weeks later, because Safir worked hard throughout
the day on a long report and finished sending it off to him
well before the deadline, the boss invited him to his place.

His house was a lodge in the same street as Maryam's. With headphones plugged into his ears, Safir was busy listening to music from his phone and making eggs in the kitchen. The boss crouched on the sofa in the living room, and the signs of authority and harshness faded away in the silence of the candle-lit gloom. Thinking about Maryam's resignation letter, in his private space, he returned to his private self. He thought about his past. When he was her age, he too was idealistic, carrying packs of Revolution in his bag. With a meagre salary, and at great personal risks, he had ventured into the remotest towns and villages of Kashmir and had brought back the live accounts of horrifying atrocities. The most memorable event was the massacre of 1993 in Bijbyor in which more than fifty people had been killed in a matter of minutes.

Seventeen years later, he reluctantly reimagined the scene: after saying their prayers on a rainy Friday afternoon, several hundred men poured out of the mosque; they gathered in the front lawn and demonstrated, chanting slogans of freedom. Soon guns were being fired from the camp across the highway; the bullets hit the bodies, the smell of blood rising, the stray dogs started barking, the soldiers were shouting, the people were running berserk, the screams of the dying drowned in the hard, pelting rain.

The boss curled up, like a woodworm on a windowsill, overlooking a floor so dark he could see almost nothing. The screams he had buried deep within him now emerged and lay in wait for him in the surrounding gloom; the screams that over all these years time had darkly distorted and transfigured

into a net of naked electric wires that would entangle him
and send shock waves through his heart.

'Give me some water,' he called Safir, drawing up his
knees to his chest.

As Safir handed him the tumbler, he closed his eyes. He
gulped down the water and let his head fall back. At the
back of his mind, unannounced, he heard the screams of
the young boys as Inspector Masoodi hit their faces with the
metal buckle of his belt.

The boss's hands trembled and his temples distended as
his eyelids puffed up. He wanted to cry but the tears did not
fall. He almost fell asleep and half an hour later when he
sat up, he saw Safir sitting on the floor by his feet. He had
dabbed his face with a wet cloth.

'My heart is heavy,' the boss said, 'and I want to tell you
something before I decide not to do so.' Safir passed him a
lit joint and listened.

'A week ago, I went into the Cantonment. There is
something called the "Tunnel" under the Wall and within
the Tunnel a place called Café Barbarica. When I went in, I
saw Inspector Masoodi. He was sitting on a chair by a glass
window, already on his fourth drink. He was mumbling
something that I could not hear clearly; the cafe was full
of loud tourists from all over: Bombay and Delhi, Chennai
and Calcutta. I slowly began to understand what Masoodi
was saying by reading his lips. He was muttering something
about how he had captured Kamran.'

'You mean the fifteen-year-old boy who we thought had
disappeared?' Safir asked.

'Yes, yes, that's the one I'm talking about.'

'Why did Inspector Masoodi capture him?'

'He beats him every night. He broke his right wrist in the last beating.'

'And why exactly did he capture him?' repeated Safir.

'Your question is both relevant and irrelevant, Safir,' the boss said, puffing hard at the weed cigarette.

'How so?' asked Safir.

'The reason for incarcerating Kamran is irrelevant to Inspector Masoodi. It is relevant to Masoodi that he captured Kamran at all. The person who imprisoned him is irrelevant to Kamran too. All that matters to the lad is that he has been captured.'

The boss fell silent and did not expand on these cryptic statements further although Safir wanted him to. Only later, from his insinuations about Kamran, did Safir conclude that during the interrogation and brutal beatings, Inspector Masoodi was pitting Kamran against Maryam's cousin Iqbal who had organized and led a protest after Ishfaq was killed. Kamran, who had come to Srinagar from his village in the south to buy an enrolment form from Kashmir University for his older brother, Shahid, had been randomly swept along in the protest march. Inspector Masoodi had arrested him along with Iqbal and a dozen other boys who had pelted the policemen blockading the demonstration.

The boss passed the joint back to Safir, who took a deep drag before releasing a plume of smoke.

Safir had been alone in the office when he heard the gunshots. It was so close, the bullets zinged past the windows that overlooked the river. He dived to the floor until the gunfire died out, and then he had crawled on all fours to peer over the windowsill towards Zero Bridge. He could see nothing; he then crept onto the balcony. Due to the power cut there were no streetlights and therefore it was too dark to see anything at all.

He went down the three flights of stairs and emerged from the rear of the building. In the deafening silence that followed the roar of gunfire, he walked in the faint starlight along the bank of the river. He was conscious of the danger of getting shot. But his feet were seized with a reckless and relentless curiosity and he kept walking.

He reasoned that the bridge and the road were at an elevation. From the top of the staircase that rose from the bank he would have a good view, although he needed to ensure that the soldier in the bunker did not catch sight of him.

He ascended the stairs gingerly and as he reached the topmost step, he trod on something soft and almost fell down in a panic. Fumbling on the steps in the dark, he realized it was a human hand. He shrieked in terror.

The hand was attached to a human body. Safir turned it over. The person was definitely dead, and in the feeble starlight the body of the youth looked pale and lifeless. His first impulse was to put as much distance between himself and this grisly scene. However, he did not want to leave the dead body there; it could be gone by the morning, fed to the river's belly.

He grabbed the corpse by the ankles and dragged it down the stairs to the bank where he stopped to catch his breath.

He then wound his arms around the body and tried to lift it. Although he got blood all over himself, the body was too heavy for him. He looked at the bridge overhead. Someone was watching him from behind the wood rails.

Facing away from the bridge and the body, he held the ankles again and lifted them. The man on the bridge, it appeared to Safir, directed the barrel of his gun towards his nape. Safir put everything he had in him to yank the corpse and haul it away with as much speed as he could muster. As he heaved and lumbered, the man on the bridge took aim at his target. Safir tightened his grip and ran, dragging the body away.

He didn't stop running until he drew closer to the office building of the *Informer*. He stopped and glanced back, sweating and gasping. No one had followed him. He wasn't sure what to do now. He pulled out his cell phone from his pocket and called Maryam.

Maryam answered his call almost on the first ring. As soon as he breathlessly outlined his predicament to her, she thought quickly and told him that the best thing would be for him to call the boss. Safir called him straightaway. The boss, sitting in Café Barbarica, immediately arrived with an ambulance and a couple of policemen who helped identify the body and convey the news to the family.

Safir waited with Wali by Kozghar's, holding Maryam. She was crying quietly but when the casket arrived floating on the shoulders of mourners, each one of them reciting, *la illaha illa Allah, la illaha illa Allah*, Maryam broke free of Safir's grip. She beat her forehead and pulled out her hair, tearing the dawn with her screams. '*Maine mahrazo, maine mahrazo*, my bridegroom, my bridegroom,' she cried.

౭

At the office, many weeks later, Safir extracted a picture of Kamran from an envelope that the boss had given him. As he looked at the aquiline nose, high cheekbones and greenish-brown eyes, he shook his head gravely. He knew only too well what was to follow: Kamran had become a rebel and would soon be cut down. He thought about Ishfaq and remembered Maryam. He felt that he had neglected her somehow. Although he had called her many times since the killing, she had steadfastly refused to answer his calls. He did not know how to reach her.

Then his mobile rang. He was surprised to see that it was Maryam.

'Can we talk?' she asked.

'Are you all right?' Safir ventured.

'We need to talk,' Maryam said.

'Where are you?'

'At home.'

'Give me a few minutes and I'll be there,' Safir replied.

On the balcony, he ran into the boss.

'Where the hell are you going so early?' he snarled.

'I'll call you later, boss,' Safir said, darting into the elevator.

As soon as the elevator touched the ground floor and the door opened, Safir strode out of the building. He ran to the edge of the river and stepped into a leaf-shaped boat.

As the boatman paddled him out to the middle, Safir kept looking towards the bunker on the bridge. He took out his mobile phone and called Maryam.

'I am coming over to your shore,' he said.

Beams of bright sunlight streamed over the poplars along the road. The façade of the house was bristling with green ivy, each leaf an oiled metal-blade.

Maryam stood outside the front door, in a trellis of shadows. Although her eyes were moist, she was standing tall.

Safir ran across the road. She gave him her hand and together they walked up the street to the boss's lodge. They went into the living room and sat on the sofa. She snuggled up against him and as he put his hand around her waist, they fell into a long hot wet kiss.

'I missed you, Maryam,' Safir whispered.

'Do you really love me?' she asked.

'What makes you think I don't?'

She wanted to tell him what had happened in the car, but he covered her lips with his lips.

'Following his death, I've had so many premonitions,' she said. 'Why don't you leave the *Informer*. Reporting means staying out late and facing such situations.'

'What will I do then?' Safir asked.

They both sat up, hands linked, facing each other.

'You could sell shoes or furniture or books,' she said. 'Or we can build something together.'

'What do you want to build with me?' He smiled. He loved her deep voice and her resonant idealism.

'How about a boutique?'

Safir nodded, although he did not know whether he could afford to leave his job. How was he supposed to survive, and pay for this very lodge that he was planning to rent from the boss so that he could live near Maryam? How was he supposed to buy books from Amazon? And save so that he could travel to the great cities of the world – Barcelona and St. Petersburg, San Francisco and Tehran?

In any case, he knew he was going to stay with Maryam that afternoon and not file any fucking reports. He knew he had to face the wrath of the boss who in turn would have to deal with the wrath of his boss in New Delhi. But he couldn't care less. A twelve-page newspaper could not be the script for his destiny. He closed his eyes, slipping his head into Maryam's lap, feeling her fingers run through his hair.

As evening approached, Safir went into the kitchen and picked up the keys. He came back to open the front door for Maryam and followed her to his black Royal Enfield which he had parked that morning in the street.

Maryam sat pillion behind Safir, holding him in an embrace. He drove down the street and to evade Wali, sped past her house over Zero Bridge. Right then a convoy of military vehicles began to issue from the Cantonement. To keep the road clear, Safir, like everyone else driving in that direction, had to press the brakes and stop before the bunker.

A structure of sandbags, Safir noticed, the bunker was wrapped in whorls of wire from which hung bright shards of broken liquor bottles. Of the soldier inside, only the whites of his eyes were visible. As a motif in the startlingly natural landscape of one of the most beautiful cities in the world, the bunker was an eyesore. It was the kind of makeshift structure one could find in street-corners, within the markets and public parks, in dilapidated houses and defunct cinemas which only the ghosts in Kashmir ever visited. However, what struck Safir then was the oddity that the appearance of the bunker presented and the sinister darkness and boredom in which the soldier seemed irredeemably cloaked. He could have been from anywhere: Jharkhand or Orissa or Mysore. Perhaps he was miserably homesick. But there he was, behind the temporary wall of sand erected in destructive opposition, where the flow of time had been altered. Within, like in a Conrad short story, time was languid, uninterrupted and murderous; without, time was rushed and fractured, a prelude to a funeral.

The convoy ended and the couple moved past the Cantonment. The soldier was now out of sight, and Safir remembered momentarily glimpsing the bunker while he was on the boat. The soldier – a shadow of the sovereign in a castle of bones – thrust the cold metal he clutched in his frost-bitten hands, beyond the wall, and into the heart of the city. The soldier, imprisoned within the choking walls, could get killed the moment he stepped out of the bunker. And the soldier had an unbounded freedom to kill on the slightest provocation. Safir could not imagine the moral landscape of such a soul – a scorching scrubland? a fatal forest? – which vacillated between the fear of getting exterminated and the terrible duty of exterminating.

The road swept around the circle. They were moving westward on the wide road flanked by huge sycamores, when in the rear-view mirror, the setting sun caught the Wall in a blood-orange light. The Wall was fortified with iron pillars placed equidistantly and had rough, uneven protrusions between its concrete cemented blocks, which could make one's fingers bleed if one brushed against them. What kind of device did one need to scratch the blocks, Safir thought. Later, when he would visit Kamran's father, he would find the answer to his question. He needed a simple device and that was the sickle with which the farmers like Abdul Rashid reaped mustard. With the sickle he needed to enter the Cantonment one dark night and scratch slowly against the Wall. He needed to keep at it until he broke the protrusions and dislodged the blocks. If only for the sake of the moon, so that it might be seen pure and whole.

In Safir's troubled imagination, the Wall, shielding the Cantonment in the east, swelled and extended out for miles, towards the northern and southern ends of Srinagar. The Wall, soaring into the sky, halved the city. For Safir, whose family lived in the east of Srinagar, the Wall cheated them of half the day by hiding the sun. For his mother, night fell a few hours after noon. There was no chance for Safir to see his home if he lodged close to where his girlfriend lived, to reside in, or cut across, both his worlds. But what terrified him more was the Wall itself, its sheer size and dimensions, colour and texture, and its strategic placement by the Cantonment kept him from even imagining where his home was.

When the Sikhs had ruled Srinagar, from 1819 to 1846, they had hanged whoever they considered a criminal among the native Muslim population from the bridges of the city. For days after these executions, the bodies hung there, shrivelled and rotting, shedding skin and flesh until only the skeletons remained.

Safir could picture the Sikh soldiers capturing Kamran in the jungle and hanging him from the bridge before dragging his mutilated corpse through the streets and into the Cantonment, where they handed the body over to the soldiers to display it on the Wall. In his mind's eye, Safir could see the vultures descending and tearing away shreds of Kamran's flesh as fecal flies buzzed around the corners of his mouth and entered his nostrils. The corpse's tongue would be distended like the tongue of a lamb suspended from the awning of a butcher's shop.

They had moved beyond the offices of the *Informer* and were almost at the Kozghar's shop, when Maryam squeezed Safir's arm, asking him to stop.

'Do you want me to come with you?' Safir asked.

'No, you go ahead and buy a kilo of fish and a quarter kilo of spinach. I have to buy some rosewater and extract for Papa's sherbets.'

She got off the bike, crossed the road and entered the shop as Safir drove a few hundred metres further and stopped at Badshah Bridge.

He parked his bike by the sidewalk and squatted in front of an old fisherwoman to haggle. Despite the heat of summer, she was wearing a woollen pheran. She wore immense bronze earrings and had braided her headgear bedecked with rings into a turban. She had a wicker basket full of minnows in front of her.

Safir bought the groceries and picking Maryam up, they soon returned to the lodge. Maryam helped him cut and clean the fish and he cooked it with tomatoes and spinach. After dinner, they made love.

2

He sat hunched in a chair on the veranda of his house. The house, facing the hills in the east, was at the edge of the village. The village was twenty-five miles south of Srinagar from where Safir had come to visit him. Behind him, he had kept the window to his empty bedroom open so that if either of his sons, Shahid or Kamran, or his wife, Murseh, were to return during the night, he'd hear their footfalls easily. They would call out to him and he would immediately run to open the entrance door downstairs to let them in.

It was late April. The mornings were cool and still but in the afternoons the air became hot and restless. He was in his usual white kameez and light cotton shalwar, although he had also thrown Murseh's shawl over his shoulders. His sleep patterns had grown erratic and last night he had barely slept at all. He felt cold and chilly. Although he was far from achieving sleep, he kept his eyes shut. His back ached and his face radiated a dull pain. His head hung as though in a reverent bow towards the hills where Kamran was suspected to be hiding in a jungle.

The sun, slanting above the roof, struck the stalks of wild grass in the courtyard with a blinding fury. From the hills, a wind had descended sharply. A page of the newspaper, made crisp by the sunlight, flapped on the table before him, waking him up.

He had read in the *Informer* about the soldiers' lusty speculations about Kamran. They had announced a bounty of ten lakh rupees on his head and proposed to capture him soon and kill him as they had killed his brother. For a moment, Abdul Rashid slipped into sleep and in that fleeting moment, his son momentarily fell out of his consciousness.

He jolted awake, opening his eyes wide. Safir appeared before him, bursting into a greeting. He told him that the front door was ajar and when he could not find anyone downstairs, he had come up.

Abdul Rashid invited him to sit down, pointing at the empty chair beside him. Murseh was not home, he said, but would he like a cup of tea, he asked.

Safir seemed like a sensitive young man like Shahid – well-spoken and well-mannered. Safir thanked him and said that he was fine without one. Abdul Rashid had never met Safir before, but he had read and followed his stories in the *Informer.* He told him so and Safir smiled.

Abdul Rashid was anticipating questions now, about his sons – one alive and one dead – but Safir asked him none.

The wind whooshed and the stalks swayed. Abdul Rashid sat back in his chair, quelling a rising sigh. Safir remained silent. In that, he was not an inquisitor like the other journalists who had visited before him. Abdul Rashid liked the way Safir was sitting with him, calm and cross-legged like his own son. He fixed his eyes on the quince tree at the end of the courtyard. Even the gusts of the gale did not distract him. However, as the force subsided, sweeping away a handful of dusty-green leaves and hurling them against the plastered façade of the house, his gaze intensified on a low branch Safir could not fathom why.

Beyond the quince tree, the mustard was in bloom. The terraced fields rose like a wide yellow ladder towards the hills. With the evening's arrival, the glazed dome of the sky became laced with light clouds.

Safir muttered something as though trying to begin a conversation. But then, he fell silent again and they continued to dwell in the silence they both seemed determined to keep. The sun sank behind the house and although the call for the dusk prayers was about to be given, there they sat, sharing the consciousness of the other's presence, saying nothing. The wind died and the fields became listlessly grey. From the village, no cackling of hens or lowing of cows could be heard.

Abdul Rashid rose, clutching Safir's arm and looked him in the eye. He told him how it was the younger son whose corpse he had imagined coming home. That day, after offering the Friday prayer in the mosque down in the village, when he returned home and sat down in the chair to read the newspaper, Murseh had given him his usual cup of tea.

'Then there under the quince tree,' Abdul Rashid said, not completing his sentence.

On the night of the last Thursday in the month of March, Shahid had said that he wanted to go to find his younger brother, Kamran, who had not been home for months. Abdul Rashid sensed danger. Was not life, the fact that we were alive, a prospect of tremendous danger? Upon seeing Shahid's determination, he did not stop him. Neither did Murseh. Instead, they gave him food in a stainless-steel container, dates and yellow rice. He left at midnight, going over the fields towards the hills. The next evening, the villagers brought a corpse home and placed it under the quince tree.

Abdul Rashid was the father. And Murseh was the mother. She had dropped her headgear and lost her sanity; she ran naked and barefoot from shrine to shrine, dribbling in deranged grief. She talked with Lal Ded, the saint in an ember-embroidered, paradisiacal pheran of fire, long dead but eternally alive; she sang senseless songs. She was far from the young maiden Abdul Rashid had seen in the fields one dazzling spring afternoon many years ago, when her pheran of diaphanous silk seemed to be on the verge of catching celestial fire and he decided, in that moment, to marry her. After Shahid, their first-born was killed, she had disappeared without a trace, leaving Abdul Rashid alone in the house.

We are tied to the rebellion with blood. Murseh's wish-knot, and seven million wish-knots on the trellised windows of Lal Ded's shrine, is one single wish for freedom woven in knots of blood.

Abdul Rashid had expected Kamran's body coming home because, after his lone visit to Srinagar, Abdul Rashid did not really know what had been done to Kamran there. And, soon after, Kamran took to arms. But that afternoon, who was it when he raised the shroud from the face of the corpse?

Not Kamran, but Shahid. His forehead had bled, leaving behind a dry red trail, around the wound the width of an index finger. Abdul Rashid had given Shahid the final bath. He lowered Shahid into the grave that the father himself had dug for his son.

The soldiers had ambushed Shahid as he handed the parcel of food to Kamran. Abdul Rashid told Safir that he often kept wondering what Shahid said to his brother a moment before the bullets hit him. What were his final words? Did he give Kamran those dates? Did the grains of soft yellow rice scatter in the air as metal tore through metal? Did Shahid hug Kamran on his mother's behalf because he had promised Murseh he would do so?

'Do you think the dead body flinched as the soldiers struck it with their guns and broke its forehead?' he asked Safir. 'What are the screams like when a dead body cries?'

Then the summons to the dusk prayers began and Abdul Rashid stopped speaking.

After a long moment of funereal silence, he said, 'It's time for prayer.'

'I want some water,' Safir said.

'The kitchen is downstairs to the left of the corridor,' Abdul Rashid said. 'I'm going to the mosque to pray.'

When Abdul Rashid returned, he led Safir to Shahid's room that was opposite the kitchen across the corridor. He switched on the lights, pointing towards the picture hanging on a wall between two long identical double-slit windows. Shahid, in a blue suit, was standing by the groom. The groom, Shahid's close friend, held the feathered crown in his hands above Shahid's head. With a sly smile, the groom squinted at Shahid; the groom's surmeh-smeared eyes had a ticklish glow and were filled with the anticipation of tasting the first delicious sip from the cup of his connubial bliss. Shahid had his arm wrapped around the groom. He had looked into the camera with the sparkling eyes and youthful charm that distinguishes a young man at the age of twenty-five. It was this youthfulness of his oval face and the sparkle of his light brown eyes that young men and women in the free nations of the world radiate. The proud posture and gait that Safir had seen in the youth parading through the streets of Paris during the revolution as depicted in the various movie adaptions of Victor Hugo's *Les Miserables*, the recklessness and fatal dignity that he had dreamt of as he prowled the streets of Srinagar at night.

Below the picture in the steep sill of the window to the right, there were two sickles. They were lying side by side, facing each other. One sickle was exactly like the other, with a curved jaw of sharp shining teeth. Abdul Rashid lifted the sickles in his hands.

Shahid helped him reap mustard, he said, handing Safir the sickle he held in his right hand. 'That was the one he used,' the father remarked. Safir smiled vindictively, thinking about the Wall.

When Safir offered to help him harvest the mustard, he nearly called him 'father'. After his prayers at the mosque, far from having a mournful demeanour and sad voice, as Safir had expected, Abdul Rashid returned radiating a stubborn dignity. He smiled as he opened the tin trunk beneath the other window. He handed Safir a polythene bag smelling of *attar* that contained a folded garment.

As Abdul Rashid moved his index finger over his own forehead, indicating the place where Shahid's forehead had been broken, Safir connected the dots. The pheran in the bag was Shahid's, the one he had worn on the day he was killed. It was a white woollen pheran, with a zip and a V-shaped collar. It had three holes in the front. One where the right sleeve met the shoulder, one on the abdomen and one right on the heart. Around each hole was a patch of dark red, but the patch around the heart was the largest. It extended to the middle of the pheran over the chest and down where it spilled into the area around the abdomen.

Abdul Rashid held the pheran up by its shoulders for Safir to take a good look at it. It had become Abdul Rashid's ritual each night to come into the room, take the pheran out of the trunk and hold it up to look at it so that the memory of his son's murder was freshly engraved in his mind.

Abdul Rashid folded the pheran and replaced it. 'For tonight, this is enough seeing,' he said.

3
A Rebel's Return

I lay motionless upon a tattered mattress on the floor, my eyes half open. The muscles in the back of my neck were stiff. My stomach roiled and my eyelids burnt. Broken images of flying glass shards from my midnight dreams flashed through my mind, like the sensations of hurt, drifting through a languorous darkness.

As I lay there longing for the peace of dreamless sleep, the door opened allowing a blinding streak of light into the room. I whimpered as I flung my arm over my eyes and cringed away as far as I could go, until my skull pressed against the wall.

When I slowly opened my eyes, Inspector Masoodi's son was standing by my feet. He was in his khaki uniform, with shoes and a belt of shining brown leather. He crouched over me.

'Your words failed,' he said.

'Don't become your father,' I whispered.

'You must be joking,' he laughed, patting his holster. He smelled of aftershave. He had nicked himself shaving, below his Adam's apple. The cut was covered in a purple clot. My eyes lingered there for a moment until the buckle of his belt glinted in my line of sight. Even in the darkness, the Sarnath sign gleamed with its three lions rearing up on their hind legs. Gaping maws and roaring, I thought, all set to pounce on me and gnaw at my bones.

'I will be sworn in as the next station-house officer today.'

'Is that what you came to tell me?'

'I am here to tell you that your words mean nothing. I am here to tell you that I will do anything to stop the likes of you from coming back to life.' He spoke with a deep conviction.

I stood up and looked directly into his eyes. 'I am not done yet,' I said softly.

'Stop raving, Ilham,' he said. 'You died many years ago, you know that. Hell, the whole world knows that.'

ॐ

Once upon a time, I led an outfit of young rebels. My area of operation was Sopor, a small town in the north. Late one autumn evening, as my comrades and I crossed an apple orchard, heading for the marketplace on the other side, we were ambushed by soldiers hiding in the thickets. All five of my men were killed instantly. I sustained the crossfire single-handedly. However, at the end, there were no bullets left in my Kalashnikov. The soldiers zeroed in on me, throwing a dagger in my direction that sunk into my back.

Half dead, the soldiers handed me over to the local police who put me into an ambulance. I was growing weaker as the bleeding wouldn't stop. The vehicle floor beneath me moved and a bluish darkness fell over me. The windowpanes became viscous and foggy, with two distant voices floating above me.

'What are we doing to Ilham, Inspector Masoodi?' asked a somewhat subdued voice.

'We take his corpse back to Srinagar,' Inspector Masoodi replied.

'But he is still alive and if we take him to the hospital, he could survive.'

'He won't make it all the way.'

Like poison, a pain slowly spread through my body. My head was throbbing and gradually going numb. 'Water, water,' I wanted to call, but my lips refused to move.

Almost an hour later, at the outskirts of Srinagar, I was hanging on to life by a thread when Inspector Masoodi asked the driver to stop the vehicle by a brook. 'Go, get some water for him,' he said.

I heard the door slide open and the man strode away. But when he returned with water in a can, originally used for diesel, and looked at me, there I lay: strangulated, my bitten tongue protruding through my teeth out of my mouth.

'What happened to Ilham, Inspector Masoodi?' the man asked.

'Poor guy. He died,' Inspector Masoodi replied.

ê

At dawn in Srinagar, the air at the graveyard on the banks of the river Jhelum was rent by the mourners' laments. A wind began to blow through the city. Inspector Masoodi walked along the curving bank, crossed the road at Badshah Bridge and entered his tall house. He went upstairs to his bedroom where Sabrin was deep asleep. He changed noiselessly and climbed into bed. He noticed that his fat, twelve-year-old son, who always slept clinging to his mother during the night, was missing. He gently shook Sabrin's shoulder.

'Where is Imran?' he asked.

'He must be somewhere in the house,' Sabrin murmured and fell asleep again.

'Foolish woman,' Inspector Masoodi grumbled.

He rose and switched on the lights. Sabrin was still snoring when he returned to the bedroom after searching the three sitting rooms in the house. He pushed open the door of the bathroom. As he stepped in, he slipped on a wet tile and knocked over a bucket filled with water with his knee.

Outside, the wind grew furious, rattling the window panes discordantly. Inspector Masoodi, spooked and suspecting ghosts in the house, ran down the stairs. He went into the kitchen, the drawing room and the guest room. 'The whore has lost me my son,' he bellowed. He returned to the kitchen and gazed out at the wind flailing about with brute force. A tremor of fear shook him, but he gathered himself quickly, clenching his fists. He darted out to the veranda, the only place in the house he had not searched.

He found three patio chairs around the iron table; the wind had shattered the glass vase, the fragments of glass and fake flowers were strewn about the tabletop. He wanted to call out for help, but he heard a human voice. He looked across at the Jhelum, ruffled and loud. He thought he was hallucinating; the sound was coming from somewhere beneath his feet.

He went down the steps into the cellar, shining the torch in his hand. At the rear of the basement he found Imran facing the wall and mumbling something.

'You devil!' shouted Inspector Masoodi. 'I looked everywhere for you.'

Imran looked immensely relieved and ecstatic. His eyes, tinted with a strange pallid shine, were overflowing with tears. He had peed in his pyjamas and his legs trembled.

'Who were you talking to?' asked Inspector Masoodi.

'Papa, can't you see him? Can't you see, Ilham?'

'Which Ilham? How do you know about Ilham?'

'Ilham, talk to my Papa,' Imran said, turning around.

'Ilham is dead,' Inspector Masoodi shouted in horror, 'Ilham is dead.'

He grabbed his son's arm in a bid to haul him into his arms, but Imran had become immobile like a hefty, frigid corpse. He did not move an inch.

'You son of the devil,' Inspector Masoodi slapped him, crying and wrapping his son in a firm embrace.

ॐ

Ever since Imran was taken away by his father, I have had no one to visit me in this low-ceilinged, narrow basement. The walls are cracked and chipped with deep cavernous shelves where bugs sing, mate and proliferate. Beneath the hay mat on the floor, the mice have dug long tunnels. Last night, I climbed the stairway leading to the door. I was enjoying a bug, chewing at its crunchy wings as the mice emerged from their tunnels and burrowed into the mattress, ripping fresh holes in the mounds of cotton. Rascals! I was furious and lashed out at them with a bamboo broom that broke as they skittered away.

I am a forbidden shadow in this space, and in the absence of light and human contact, I feel an almost lethal contentment. The walls contain me. I'm sick with their warmth. My head hits the ceiling. I scream, desperate, my arms flailing. This is the point when I want throw myself out of here.

That morning as Imran, who calls himself Inspector Masoodi now, left, I followed him. However, like his father, he shut the door on me and latched it from outside. I sat on the top step, ruminating on the wings of the bug I had caught. I regretted the whole thing – our first meeting, how I had won him over, how he had believed me and vowed that he would never become his father.

I was so angry that I turned around and punched the wooden door. I hit the door so hard that one of the fingers fell off my right hand. A finger without flesh. Picture what that looks like. Three thin bones one on top of the other. A piece of fragile artwork.

My finger fell on the topmost stair and walked down like a human baby with legs. As soon as it reached the floor, it ran after the mice. I ran after it. My finger was giving me a hard time, but I finally caught it as it emerged from a burrow. I put it back on my hand.

I was at the door again. I hit it so hard this time that all my fingers fell off. But it was all good, I tell you, it was all good. The latch on the other side fell off.

I roamed the city that entire day, but finding that no one could hear, see or touch me, I became miserable. In the evening, I stood on Zero Bridge, looking at the river Jhelum. It was full and green and small boats floated on it. It was the river in which I had bathed and laughed as a child, playfully splashing water onto my friends. I wondered whether I could at least generate a ripple in the river if I jumped into it. But with the sun disappearing behind the Himalayas and the darkness falling over the city, it seemed unlikely. Srinagar was both deaf and blind to me. I had an overwhelming urge to return to the basement, ensconce myself on the mattress and sleep among the skittering mice.

I walked to the end of the bridge. I noticed a soldier inside the bunker and decided to explore the Cantonment instead of heading back to the cellar.

Inspector Masoodi was seated on a sofa in Café Barbarica, sipping a brandy and enjoying the opulent ambience. Noisy tourists were window-shopping and gazing at the souvenirs whittled from bones and wood. I noticed a wooden hand with missing fingernails. An authentic-looking ribcage missing its mid ribs. There was also a magnificent elbow, suspended from the ceiling by a skin-coloured string.

Inspector Masoodi finished his drink and stepped out into the Tunnel. I followed him as he walked to the furthermost end and went into a dark prison cell where two young boys were lying on the cold, stone floor covered in spit and stinking of faeces. He tapped his cane against their feet.

'Fucking miscreants,' he shouted. Opening their eyes, they stood up, groggy and terrified.

'Kamran, take this,' he said to one of them, 'or I empty my gun into your head.'

As Kamran took the tweezers from his hand, Inspector Masoodi unclasped his trouser belt. He thrashed the other boy's back with the buckle-end. He grabbed his arm and ripped off the sleeve of his shirt. 'Pluck out Ishfaq's hair,' he shouted at Kamran. Kamran took a second to respond and Inspector Masoodi started to beat him.

As I watched this scene play out through the bars on the window, I realized that it made me neither sad nor angry.

As Kamran collapsed onto the floor, I entered the prison cell and stood behind Inspector Masoodi. He grabbed Ishfaq by the scruff off his neck, ripping the collar off his shirt as well. He produced another set of tweezers from his trouser pocket and slapped Ishfaq before stabbing him in the shoulder with the forceps.

'*Atto Khudayo*,' Ishfaq cried. O God.

'This is the fucking fate of a stone-thrower,' Inspector Masoodi spit out.

He grabbed Ishfaq's shoulder, grinding the tweezers into his flesh while simultaneously yanking the hair on his scalp.

Kamran sat up looking horrified. He covered his eyes with his palms and began to weep.

'I'll thrust these tweezers into your mother's vagina if you ever organize a protest against me or even think of hurling a rock at me.'

'Please let me go … please—,' Ishfaq cried.

ॐ

I went into the house. There was a copper pitcher filled with water in the kitchen sink. I climbed onto the sink and peed into the pitcher.

Then I went upstairs. Yasmin, Inspector Masoodi's wife, was in her bedroom. Her baby, very little and very soft, just like a mewling mouse, was in her lap.

The baby boy gazed around the room in wonderment as his mother suckled him. Yasmin then lay down beside him, comforting him, until they both fell asleep.

I wedged myself between mother and child and lay by her side, looking at her round breast with its taut, dark nipple. I wanted to suck on it. I put my lips around her nipple but stopped. Although she was still asleep, the child behind me woke up. His father's son, he could see me. I drew him close and picking him up, took him into the basement. This time, I was not going to preach. This time, I was going to strangle him like his grandfather had strangled me.

I put my hand around his little neck. My fingers tickled him and he laughed. Good God! Is there any sound more pleasing than the sound of a child's laughter?

I took him back upstairs and placed him on the edge of the bed and lay down by Yasmin. I took her breast in my hand and drew her nipple into my mouth. I sucked at it and stole all her milk.

That night, when Inspector Masoodi returned home, I was burrowed in the mattress, playing with a bug I had caught. The finger that had left me was chasing after the mice. Then I heard the child crying. Inspector Masoodi, drunk and thirsty, shouted at Yasmin to bring him water from the kitchen. 'Ha, ha!' I laughed.

4
The Souvenir

~❦~

My father was my first teacher. Each morning, when I stood with other students in the school ground, my hands tied beneath my heart in prayer, he would stand on the veranda and say, 'God is the light of the heavens and earth.'

After school, I walked home, my satchel slung on my back and my hands deep in my pockets. I stopped by the curb, in front of Shah-e-Hamdan's shrine. The yellow hazard sign, the word 'DANGER' inscribed in large, black capital letters beneath the universal emblem of the skull and crossbones on a metal sheet, was nailed to a wooden pole to flag up the existence of potentially dangerous electric cables.

I looked at the sign and an unnamed fear seized me. The street, cheery with the honking of cars and scooters, suddenly felt desolate and empty. The sky, filled with bright light, grew bleak.

Day after day, I had passed by this signpost, without raising my head or giving it a second thought. But on that day, I gritted my teeth, gulped down the saliva in my drying mouth, clenched my fists inside my pockets and stared into the eyeless sockets of the grinning skull. When I am dead, I thought, my body will be buried. My skin and flesh will eventually rot away. But how can death be possible when, in this moment, I feel so alive. How can this happen to me when I am standing here on this June afternoon in the city of Srinagar, me with my limbs, feet and head all intact.

I took a step back and, without completely understanding why, I picked up a jagged rock from the road and heaved it at the sign with all the strength that I could muster.

I missed the board entirely and the rock soared high and hit a pigeon perched on the crossbar of the pole. The bird crashed down on the curb.

The city and all its traffic ought to have screeched to a halt as people gathered around the dying pigeon in solemn silence. But no one stopped or even noticed. I was left standing with the skull sign over my head and the dying pigeon near my feet, and this petrified me. It was time for Father to return home along that very street. I dreaded his arrival at the scene. I looked at the pigeon squirming in its death throes, a tiny droplet of shining blood swelling on its neck.

'Look at what you've done!' I could just about see Father shaking me as he glared accusingly at me.

I heard steps approaching me from behind. I felt a crushing guilt. Without turning around to confirm whether it was him, I ran away.

Minutes later, when I reached home, I was breathless and miserable. Mother walked out of the front door. 'What's the matter, Tariq?' she asked.

'Never am I going into the shrine with Father,' I hollered. 'Never again!'

ॐ

Father went to the shrine every afternoon like clockwork. Bearing a rosary in his right hand, he faced the house-shaped tomb that was covered with a black velvet drape embroidered with the verses of the Qur'an. With an expression of abject subservience on his white-bearded face, he fingered each bead in turn. *Ya Shah-e-Hamdan, Ya Shah-e-Hamdan*, he intoned, naming the saint. 'If you chant the saint's name with a pure heart, he'll hear you and call your name in response,' he said.

His footsteps held a deep, rhythmic silence as he came into the courtyard. His eyes shone with an ethereal light and his lips continued to murmur praises for the saint. He put his hand into his side pocket, withdrew a handful of rice grains and sprinkled them on the plaza. Flocks of pigeons descended from the roof immediately.

When the war came to Srinagar eighteen years ago, his visits to the shrine were followed by long walks through the city. He picked up the shells of the bullets from where the guns had been fired by the soldiers. He brought these shells home and hid them in a cache.

I did not know about this. It was only last week, when I turned eighteen, that Mother told me. She also said that she had asked Father what made him do it. 'I don't want Tariq to see the bullet shells when he goes out to play,' he had replied.

Father had faith. His eyes were frighteningly placid. He was not riddled with doubt like I was. The shape of a rice grain resembled the shape of a bullet, I thought. In Father's absence, I often pictured the grains of rice turning into bullets, clogging little mouths, choking the pigeons dead.

§

I looked for the shells in the morning and found them in a small rexine bag under the staircase in the corridor. I carried the bag to my room on the third storey and unzipped it.

The shells clattered onto the floor, buzzing and scattering like hornets as the afternoon sun that streamed in through the open window illuminated them. I ran downstairs to the semi-dark corridor and rummaged under the staircase until I found Father's aluminium toolbox. I raked through the assortment of nuts and bolts, and quickly retrieved a hammer, a string, a couple of sharp nails and an iron brick.

I ran back upstairs and scooped up the shells. I placed each one on the iron brick and hammered a nail into it until it pierced the metal. I strung them together on the string. Then I hammered two nails at each end of the wooden lintel over the window and hung up the rosary.

The neighbourhood was poor and grimy. Amidst a cluster of small houses, there was an empty plot of land. One evening, when I was about five, the rebels moved into the house that stood there then. It was a tall, concrete building with strong brick walls and white, glass-paned windows. Of the night that followed, I remembered crouching beneath the staircase with Father's arm wrapped around my head. In the crossfire, the bullets perforated our roof. The explosions of light and sound during that long fire-fight made the ground shake and rumble. The soldiers fired mortar shells, tearing down the walls of the house. The reek of gunpowder and charred flesh sent me into a paroxysm of coughing.

I fingered the beads over my window, wondering whether the shells I was touching with my fingertips now were the ones that encased those bullets. I pulled at the ends of the rosary to get a wider view. I looked through it at the entirety of the plot; the spot in the middle where the building once stood was oddly desolate and blank. The clover growing on the outer fringes of the base had failed to enclose the blackened rocks of the ruin.

ॐ

One afternoon, a few weeks later, as I entered the kitchen, Father said, 'Tariq, you will not step out of the house.'

'Why not, Father?' I asked.

'Those who don't believe in Shah-e-Hamdan should not step out of their houses during curfew,' he said.

'The shrine is just around the corner,' I argued, 'and there are no soldiers on our street.'

I rose on my toes to peer out of the rear window and pointed to a man on the street through the glass pane on top. Father stood up on the floor and craned his neck to look at the man's head. He shrugged, opening the door of the cabinet reluctantly. He gave me a handful of rice in a polythene bag.

I grabbed the bag with a grin and hurried out to collect my bicycle from the veranda before he could change his mind.

'Come help me soften the soil,' Mother beckoned me with a trowel from amidst the *hakh* plants in the vegetable patch.

'I am off to the shrine,' I replied.

'Why today of all days?' she grumbled as she bludgeoned a hard lump of earth. 'You've always refused to go to the shrine for as long as I can remember.'

'To feed the pigeons,' I quipped.

'You should make sure to have your ID card with you.'

I patted my breast pocket that held the card which she had forced me to have laminated. I fastened the rice bag to the handlebars and wheeled the bicycle down the corridor, down the porch steps and out onto the street. I smiled at the passing pedestrians although their furtive glances filled me with trepidation. I surveyed the street as far as my eyes could see. There wasn't a soldier in sight. I mounted my bicycle and pedalled, keeping to the shade by the line of the shuttered shops on my right.

As I approached the hazard sign, I espied a flock of grey rock pigeons sunning on the sloping roof of the shrine. I leaned my bicycle against the gate of the shrine and pushed the gate open. A fat, unkempt soldier thundered down to me, his waterproof lumberjack boots with their thick, deep-rutted soles thudding on the tarmac.

'Show me your ID,' he barked. His eyelids were puffy and a frizzy beard covered his bloated face.

I quickly extracted it from my pocket.

'Don't you know that the city is under curfew?' he snatched the card from my hand.

'Yes, I know.' I could smell the cheap rum on his foul breath.

'Then why did you venture out of your house?'

'For my father's sake,' I replied.

'Your father?' the soldier repeated.

'He feeds the pigeons at the shrine,' I said tersely. I couldn't bring myself to explain to this callous creature that Father hadn't been eating well because he was worrying about the pigeons. It would only exacerbate the situation.

The soldier scrutinized my ID, flicking a glance at me to check that the picture was really me. I was fairly sure that he was going to beat me and kick me with those gargantuan shoes. Then I heard wings flapping. Damn the pigeons, I thought. It was because of them that I was now in this pickle.

The soldier slapped my shoulder. 'Go feed the pigeons,' he said. I unhitched the bag from the bicycle's handlebar and raced down the stone stairs to the bottom of the enclosure. I stood within the square stone plaza streaked white and brown with pigeon droppings. The bronze tip of the spire gleamed above the three-tiers of the green, shingled roof. The pigeons circled the spire in perfectly co-ordinated flight patterns, their wings clapping exultantly against the sky.

I scattered the grains across the plaza. The pigeons fluttered down to peck at them on the stone. My errand completed, I stepped out of the gate to hurry back home when the soldier called me back.

'Please, sir, may I go now?' I asked nervously.

'No,' he tucked my ID into his hip-pocket, 'you cannot.'

'Please?'

'Stand over there,' he pointed to the fence.

He followed me to the place that he had indicated and thrust his gun into my hands.

'Now turn around and place the gun barrel there,' he ordered, pointing to a gap in the metal grille.

I squatted on my haunches and did as I had been told. He placed a heavy hand on my head and grasped a tuft of my hair – like it was grass – using his hold to direct my eyes to the plaza.

'Shoot, motherfucker!' he shouted, yanking at my hair.

I closed my eyes in terror as my heart pounded loudly. I was petrified.

'SHOOT, MOTHERFUCKER!'

I shuddered and opened my eyes. I pressed the trigger. On the plaza, two pigeons dropped dead.

'Good shot,' he said, his gaze fixed on the square. 'Now go fetch the hunt.'

I surreptitiously palmed the bullet shell that had fallen by my foot as I stood up. Slipping it into my trouser pocket, I turned around and returned the soldier's gun before walking back slowly to the plaza.

When I looked back, I saw the bearded soldier surrounded by other soldiers who had rushed out upon hearing the gunshot. The barrels of their guns were levelled at me, but the soldier must have assured them that there was nothing to worry about because they slunk back to their patrol stations.

The pigeons that had flown away had returned to finish their meal, wholly ignoring the two dead birds lying there, belly up, with their stiff pink legs pointing skyward.

I walked to the centre of the plaza, but the pigeons ignored me as well and did not fly away in fright.

As I knelt to cup each flaccid belly in my palms, I looked into the dark interior of the shrine. I longed to rest my eyes on something that would give me assurance. But there was no such thing hovering inside. All I could discern faintly in the dark were the gilded letters of the Qur'an on the drape hanging from a wall.

The soldier babbled merrily as he looked at the little corpses. He extracted a coiled metal wire and a dagger from his hip-pocket.

'Hold this end,' he ordered and cut a section of the wire. He tied the bodies together by making a knot around their legs. He slung the bodies over his shoulder, holding on to the other end of the wire. 'I'll skin them and roast them,' he said smiling.

'May I go now?' I snapped and without waiting for his reply, I spun around and marched off towards my bicycle.

'Take this,' he said. I straddled the bike and wheeled it around with a foot on the pedal, snatching my ID from his hand as I rode away.

At home, I saw Father and Mother sitting worriedly beside each other in the corridor. 'You came back,' Mother said tearfully.

'Why are you sitting here and not in the kitchen?' I asked as she gathered me in a tight embrace.

'We heard a gunshot and thought—' Father couldn't complete his sentence.

'I heard it, too,' I said, unable to meet his anxious gaze and looking at Mother instead.

'We were worried,' she said.

'A million thanks to Shah-e-Hamdan,' Father raised prayerful palms heavenward, 'that you are safe.'

'I'm fine, Father,' I said and clasped his hands. I handed him the glass of water that Mother fetched from the kitchen.

As he calmed down, Mother asked: 'You must be hungry?'

'You start ladling rice,' I said, 'I'll be back in a minute.' I ran upstairs and quickly went to the window. I took out the bullet shell from my pocket and held it up between my forefinger and thumb. Then I dropped it on the floor.

I returned after my meal and retrieved the piece of metal. I drilled it and added it to the rosary.

5
Rosy

❦

That autumn morning in Rasool Mir College in Anantnag, four thousand hands released two thousand pigeons, and four thousand grey wings rose towards the tall, bright-blue sky clattering in applause. Gold-coloured dust was roused by the feet, stamping and dancing. My heart rose as well in the storm of rapture, whirling like a dervish, although I stood rooted to the spot at the edge of the lawns as I had listened to your astonishing address. Nuzhat, rapt and attentive, had also watched you throughout one long, arduous hour. As your speech ended and your admirers dispersed, although she felt hot and thirsty, she refused to leave without me. However, I somehow persuaded her to. The moment she left, Nadim appeared with a note in his hand, a note written in your handwriting.

As he handed it to me, I caught the sight of the last line: *One day I'll take my Rosy across the river Jhelum to my home, in the middle of an endless pasture.* I was about to unfold the note and read the whole thing when Nadim fell to his knees and began to weep bitterly. Up until then, I had thought of him as a brawny lad and a bonafide bully. I always thought that bullies were conscious of their choice and role, and couldn't be broken easily or trusted beyond a point. However, seeing Nadim sobbing and pleading like this made me adjust my compass. I pretended to be clueless and asked him what the matter was.

He began his sorry tale, ruefully and hesitantly. A few months ago, on a hot summer day, he had got into a bus in Bijbyor after working from morning till noon at my father's shoe shop. He was on his way here when, in Khanbal, a pretty girl got on the crowded bus. She stood in the aisle near Nadim, smiling at him. She was in a black silk abaya, covered from neck to toe, but her headscarf kept slipping from her head onto her shoulders.

As they reached Dak Bungalow, the conductor, precariously hanging from the door, called to the driver to stop. The driver slammed the brakes and Nadim edged closer to the girl. As more passengers pressed their way in, Nadim pressed against her. She threw him an annoyed glance. This aroused him, her anger. The bus went on over the bumpy road, and Nadim pressed his shoulder against hers. He touched her waist and back with his fingertips and nudged her breast with his elbow. She was sweating, uncomfortable and furious. She wanted to turn around and slap him so hard that all his teeth would come loose. But he was not the only one cramming her and holding her arms from swinging.

There were other men: an old, pot-bellied man, a coat-wearing clerk with thin-rimmed glasses and a sheepish smile, and a long-bearded man with a fierce face.

Nadim rubbed his crotch against her butt. She spun around and thrust her hand into his chest. But in the great surrounding weight, he did not budge. He stood pressed against her, sinking his chin into her shoulder.

As they crossed the river Jhelum over Khanbal Bridge, he got stiff. He was about to thrust his cock between her buttocks when the conductor called again. The bus stopped and the other three men around the young girl moved forward in the aisle with great difficulty and disembarked. She got out after them, still two miles away from the college. She was so terrified that she did not dare board another bus.

I did not mention this to you before but do you know who the girl was? Our own Nuzhat. The day this happened, after finishing her zoology class, when she came out into the corridor, she grabbed me by the edge of my scarf.

'Are you okay, Nuzhat?' I asked.

She stood speechless for a long time. And then her words came tumbling out as she told me what had happened, her eyes filling with tears.

Nadim would not know that; how could he? As he was telling me his version, he omitted many details. I remembered the feeling of betrayal in Nuzhat's eyes, as though all of Kashmir had failed her. I am a woman and Nuzhat is my dearest friend. I felt her rage, her desperation, her hurt. But here was Nadim, down on his knees, begging for forgiveness. I was not sure of what he was up to and did not know how to feel about him at the moment. He was now fully aware of how much Nuzhat meant to me and probably how close Showkat was to you, Jamshid.

I told him to go away, but he would not. And when I mentioned your name saying I would talk to you, his face remained sorrowful, but his eyes filled with a subtle light. He was not worried that Nuzhat was Showkat's sister, even if he was the commander of the JKLF that was dreaded by the entire army stationed in our district. What concerned him, he told me before going away, was losing your trust and friendship.

'I can give my life for Jamshid,' he told me, 'in a heartbeat.'

I was moved by his words. He left me in a moral dilemma. I waited for you, alone, at the spot you mentioned in your note. I stood there in the hot sun, facing the brick wall that separated the lawns from Cheeni Chowk, blocking my view of Western Hosiery where I buy my things and those mist-white bottles of perfume for you.

To distract Nuzhat, I had proposed a visit to the store that day and she had agreed. As soon as my geography class ended, we walked out of the eastern gate into Cheeni Chowk.

It was a hot and dusty day in mid-July. We walked on a sidewalk over broken cobblestones, against an unbroken stream of men, pushing us against the military bunker protruding from the street corner. The soldier behind the dark olive mesh of threads stuck his tongue out and, mumbling something lewd, licked his lips.

Nuzhat grabbed my arm, shouting in his face, 'When it comes to women, you scumbags are the same everywhere.'

We walked past a row of carts, loaded with melons – cut open and bleeding profusely – and mounds of cheap socks, until we reached the store. It was in the middle of a long row of shops covered in layers of dust. It was the only shop in Cheeni Chowk with a glass front.

The owner was a jovial, middle-aged fellow, seemingly untouched by the invisible war-worms that bred grief and distrust in our stomachs and livers. However, as we ascended the three steps into the store, Qadir Suth went pale behind his counter. I wondered what was bothering him until Nuzhat turned and whispered, 'Look! It's my brother.'

I turned too and there I saw the man. He was of your stature. He was standing very close to me with his Kalashnikov slung across his shoulder. He greeted me and his sister, and patting Qadir Suth on the arm, told him not to panic.

The first impression I had of Showkat, I must say, was one of solemnity. He was wearing a bright, sky-blue shalwar kameez and white sneakers. His eyes were deep-set and defiant. His forehead was ponderous and calm like the river Jhelum the morning after the last spring rains. It did not bother him that there were soldiers walking outside on the street; he acknowledged his nearness to death. And by virtue of that difficult acknowledgment, he seemed to have pushed beyond the bounds of human mortality. If you looked closely, a fierce light gleamed in the depths of his eyes. The light a white-hot rod of iron achieves when it is about to burn itself out and morph into something else altogether. His gestures were grave, and in his words, there was finality – what a terrible finality it was. Later, contemplating the quality of his tone, I would be reminded of your dazzling speech. I wonder now, during all your secret meetings where Showkat chose you as the leader of the Jammu Kashmir Youth Front, whether it was from him that you picked up the art of firing words with velocity.

'Tell Mother that I am fine,' Showkat said. 'I will not die before I have taken my revenge and cut Major S's hand. The same hand with which he seized my hair, while making me lick the graffiti.'

Showkat probably noticed that Nuzhat was upset and wanted to say something, but he forestalled her words by quickly putting a five-hundred rupee note in her hand before vanishing through the back door.

Qadir Suth looked like he was about to faint. He gulped down some water from a big bottle, wiped his damp brow and took a deep breath now that Showkat was gone. We bought chemises from him and left.

Although I did not ask Nuzhat, as soon as we went back to the college she told me that her brother had deep gashes in his tongue. Now that she had brought it up, I asked how that had happened. She then went on to tell me the entire story. Two years ago, Showkat was a grocer. One morning when Nuzhat had left home for college, in the marketplace, Mir Bazar, where she waited for the bus, she suddenly saw Showkat, his face pressed against the cemented wall of his shop, his back to her. Six soldiers encircled him. Showkat was moving his head up and down. What was he doing? Nuzhat wondered. He was licking the wall of his own shop, his tongue following the letters of graffiti: JKLF. The soldiers kicked Showkat as he lapped at the letters. They smashed the shelves of the shop and threw out cabbages and neatly tied bunches of spinach onto the street. They broke the crates of apples and oranges in front of the shop and then moving inside, they shattered the glass jars filled with spices and threw out biscuit packets and gunny bags of beans and rice on the road.

'They made him wipe the letters with his tongue?' I interjected.

'With his tongue,' Nuzhat affirmed, 'until it began to bleed.'

What a horrible incident, I shuddered. Thinking about Showkat, his stature and his solemnity, I was disappointed with Qadir Suth for behaving like a coward. However, later that evening at home in Bijbyor, as I reclined on my bed while outside it had grown overcast and a dark wind stirred the willow groves outside my window, I imagined him alone inside his shop.

'I should lower the shutter,' Qadir Suth thought when, with the first flash of lightning and rumble of thunder, the electricity went out. He switched on his electric torch and put it on the counter. All the other shops along that street were shuttered and the carts were abandoned and empty. To fend off the eerie silence that had suddenly descended on the street, he whistled tunelessly and opened the drawer to occupy his mind by totting up his profits for the day. As he built a wad of the notes, a jeep came speeding up and screeched to halt in front of his shop.

The soldiers jumped out and barged inside.

'Was Showkat here during the day?' Major S demanded stridently.

Qadir Suth was mute with fear. His hands trembled and the bills slipped through his fingers and cascaded to the floor.

Major S grabbed him by the collar and slapped him. 'Was Showkat here during the day?' he repeated.

Qadir Suth nodded timorously.

'Why didn't you inform me?'

Qadir Suth mumbled incoherently and Major S slapped him again and inserted the barrel of his pistol into the terrified shopkeeper's mouth.

'I'll kill you right now,' he threatened.

Qadir Suth's heart pounded. Major S used the butt of the gun to slap his jaw.

'Atto, Khudayo!' Qadir Suth cried. O God!

'*Maderchod*,' Major S shouted. Motherfucker. He pistol-whipped him repeatedly until Qadir Suth's head thudded on the counter, his cheek torn and bleeding.

'Put him here,' Major S indicated the floor at the entrance of the shop. The soldiers immediately pounced on the shopkeeper and dragged him to the front.

'Raman, give me your rifle,' Major S commanded. 'Showkat must understand the consequences for acquiring weapons from Pakistan to wage a war against me.'

Major S carried Raman's steel-barrelled rifle to the sidewalk and stood gazing at the glass, eyeballing its thickness.

'Raman, get the petrol,' he said. 'Come on, hurry up!'

Raman quickly brought a can of petrol from the jeep. As the other soldiers stood around Qadir Suth's prostate form, their guns pointing to his head, Raman sprinkled petrol on the shelves stacked with clothes and bales of fabric. He even doused the flower-printed, summer frock hanging from the ceiling.

'That's enough, boys,' Major S ordered. The soldiers trooped out and Major S shattered the glass front of the shop with a tremendous blow of the gun's metal barrel. Glass slivers rained down on Qadir Suth's cringing body on the floor. Although he heard the jeep drive away and saw the flicker of flames around him, he felt paralysed and numb with terror. As the smoke started suffocating him, he spluttered and coughed. He slowly crawled out, stumbling down the steps.

ॐ

As soon as we returned to the campus, I asked Nuzhat whether she would tell Showkat about Nadim. Her face flushed. I could tell at a glance that she had second thoughts about confiding in her brother and I did not press her about it.

Do you think I ought to have, Jamshid? I wonder now how Showkat would have responded. Men conscious of their mortality know the value of time. I have told you every detail and I leave you to be the final judge.

Nuzhat, who had seen me talking to Nadim, seemed upset by this and left without saying goodbye. I wanted to run after her and tell her that I was on her side, but she was already out through the gate. I felt miserable about this until I looked around at the posters on the walls fencing the lawns. They were all close-ups of your face and they cheered me up. The fire in your eyes was muted but unquenchable. Your

nose, an ascending Himalayan ridge. Your smile, captivating
and prophetic. Across it, in a splash of red ink, was the widely
spaced word extending from one end of your jaw to the other:
'FREEDOM'. The letter 'R' hung from your lower lip in a
weird, sensual way. You are the face of our revolution, a face
behind which rebels like Showkat unite, assimilate and act.

The eastern wall on the side of Cheeni Chowk was a fifty-
metre-long and three-metre-high brick wall that was webbed
with thin gashes. Rumour had it that this damage had been
caused by a grenade attack carried out by Showkat himself.
Despite its dilapidated condition, the wall continued to
create the semblance of a shield saving us, the inhabitants of
the campus, from the fulminating outside world.

I waited for you. I sweated as the sun blazed over my
head. I turned in one quick beat of heart, opening my eyes,
and there you were. I am having a vision, I thought. The
clarity of your eyes, the way you looked at me. I am ever
so grateful to Baba for finding you in that village seventeen
years ago and bringing you home.

I apologize for pinching your finger yesterday during
lunch while handing you the bowl of water. When I came
back up afterwards, I walked inside the bathroom. I thought
of you when I undressed and stood in front of the mirror as
I was getting ready to take a bath. An erotic warmth spread
through me as the hot water coursed down the slope of my
shoulders. I fantasized you standing behind me in the shower,
your hands cupping my bare breasts.

At night, I lay on my bed, but I could not sleep. The
whole night went by, my eyes wide open, filled with the

longing to see you. At dawn, groggy and tired, I took one pill from the new strip of sedatives I had hidden in the drawer. I fell asleep and woke up at noon, but I did not leave my bed. Half-awake, sedated into a state of willed dreaming, I looked at the clean white curtain, stained with the flowers of blood.

I was on the veranda. The nozzle hung above the geraniums, and common sense told me to look across the long lawn, towards the cow byre. Beneath the raised, rust-brown wings of its roof, set brilliantly on fire by the April sun that noon, my eyes searched the dim interior of the room, and peering within I glimpsed the cave of my childhood whose winding solitary alleys I was tempted to tread again. The water from the numerous pores drizzled over the pink petals. Wispy white roots drank their fill until they were soggy and satiated, the water soundlessly penetrated the hearts of the soil particles, suffusing the empty spaces in between, and pushing up and away over the round rim of the pot, a deluge bubbling and swelling in a dam of dirty, brown water, a multitude of trickles descending to touch my bare, tingling toes. 'Heeeesh!' I whispered, glimpsing you in the window across the lawn. I lost my grip of the hose handle. Fresh from my bath, the white crown of the towel around my head came loose and my wet hair tumbled free as the water sprayed out on the hard, white marble floor.

Baba slammed the kitchen door downstairs and cleared his throat loudly as he stepped into the hall across the corridor packed with murids. I shook my head and realized I was still abed. However, the room over the cow shed, I must proceed to tell you, was once my playground and my sanctuary. Every Friday afternoon, Mama smuggled me there as soon as the men of the house went away to pray. She liked to smoke jajeer and there was none in our house. She would leave me behind, latching the door from the outside, and go to the neighbours' houses.

I played for hours with numerous stuffed dolls and drew with crayons. Those dolls and crayons and snow-white stashes of paper were my first gifts from Papa during the early days when he still loved my mother and me.

It saddened me to see Mama crushed beneath the weight of her sorrow. Papa had fallen in love again with Nadim's mother, Misreh, after her husband passed away in an accident. He smelled of her shirmals every time he came home. I wouldn't have known about this had they not had a huge row one night.

'You stink of tobacco,' Papa accused.

'You won't like it even if I wash myself over and over again because you are used to the smell of shirmals,' Mama replied.

I hated Papa for cheating on my mother until I grew up and understood that the reason he could not even think of asking Baba's permission to marry Misreh before he had to marry Mama was because she was a baker's daughter, and a Ganai – a lower caste by the standards of our family. I don't hate Papa anymore, not with the intensity with which I hated him that night, although I think he could have rebelled like you and I would have in that scenario. In his undying affection for Misreh, in his inability to put an end to that affair, I would later find the root of my complicity.

My father had been sleeping with Nadim's mother and that day when he asked for my clemency on the college lawns I might have harboured the feelings of a sister for him. I felt guilty and more so because Mama was and continued to be sad. She disappeared for hours on end to smoke jajeer in the neighbours' houses and had started to cough up blood.

'Mama, you must stop this,' I told her.

'Not until I have destroyed the cold grief sitting in my lungs, my child,' she retorted.

ҫ

Shireen Kochak was Qadir Suth's only niece. Her stately looking father with the disproportionately large, pockmarked nose brought her along to show her to Baba a few weeks before your arrival at Syed Manzil. Although Ramzan Kochak was one of the richest men in the Anantnag district and owned most of the shops in Cheeni Chowk, Shireen was in rags. He had banned her from meeting with her lover, Farhad Ahangar, who was his driver.

Shireen had abandoned both Rasool Mir College and food and had become emaciated and epileptic. She had sworn off bathing and make-up until her death or until they returned her lover to her. The stench that rose from her armpits and crotch was rancid. She raved in the dead of the night and at times when she heard her father's Maruti 800 swishing through Cheeni Chowk, she sang in a sweet albeit desolate voice, frantically running from window to window in the room on the second storey where her father had locked her up. Despite her unkempt hair and fingernails, her eyes remained beautiful and inexpressibly sad.

I saw her in the corner of the hall, seated in front of Baba, humming the most popular Rasool Mir song:

> *I tremble I'll fall dead*
> *My hope has fled*
> *My yar, the one I adore*
> *I don't see him anymore*

'Stop, you devil,' Baba scolded her.

Shireen's dilated pupils flickered for an instant before she burst into hysterical laughter and tears coursed down her face.

Baba dropped an *isband* in the firebowl before him. The dried white mallows burnt and white wisps of bitter smoke rose. Baba whispered to his rosary, holding her gaze.

'Go away,' he shouted, 'otherwise, I'll smoke you out of here.'

Shireen stopped weeping and her eyes gained focus. Perspiration beaded her brow and she trembled. She fainted into her father's arms who looked worriedly at Baba.

'The jinn has left the girl,' Baba said. 'It wasn't a stubborn one.' He scribbled verses of the Qur'an on a small piece of paper with a fountain pen and folded it.

'Put this in a locket and put the locket around the girl's neck,' he instructed Ramzan Kochak.

The grateful father returned to the hall with a bag of figs. 'The *taweez* is working and the girl is cured of all her memories,' he said. 'She has agreed to marry my nephew. And I want *you* to perform the nikah next week.'

Baba smiled and asked Mama to put the bag on the top shelf in the kitchen – the shelf I cannot reach even today. It was from that bag that you stole a fig for me. As it was raw, you cut it open with your teeth, and put the hard rinds of green-and-pink flesh into my hands. When I chewed them, my mouth burnt and blistered and my lips swelled up. I wept and the whole house came to know.

I was watching you from the veranda as they took you out. Papa passed the willow switch to Baba who did not pause to even think before administering the punishment. Turning a deaf ear to my protests that you had stolen merely a fucking fig, and that it was only for me, he flogged you mercilessly as the sun blazed down into the courtyard. When the switch whipped across your face, a bright welt of blood welled up on your forehead.

A few months later, the news came in hushed whispers that Shireen, who had only feigned convalescence, had killed herself by drinking a bottle of rat poison on the eve of her wedding. As they lowered her bloated body into the grave, her father broke down. He leaned onto Qadir Suth and said, 'Had I known that the whore loved the measly driver so much, I would have agreed to everything she asked.'

I find it hard to believe that Baba, who raised, groomed and educated you, is sending you away now when you are ready to lead us to the path of freedom. With him around, we won't be able to meet during your fleeting sojourn at Syed Manzil.

I have never seen you scowl. Ever. However, that afternoon, as I waited for you and you deliberately dawdled to our rendezvous, your forehead was furrowed and your eyes were dazed. You seemed lost and distracted.

You foresee it all: the light and the darkness. You are a miracle of memory draped in the folds of eloquence. I have plunged with you into this scalding river whose brilliant waters I want to embrace without caring whether we'll reach the shore. I don't care that my actions will sully my family's reputation. The world is cruel; it ties us to the stanchions of caste. I will never cease to love you. I am furious to be tethered like this. I want to detonate the skulls by planting rose-bombs and geranium-grenades in the putrid, filthy brains of Baba, Papa, Qadri, Masoodi, Suharwardi, Kubravi, Naqshbandi, Bukhari, Haqani, Mubarki, Geelani. I want to burn down the edifice of the whole damn society who believe that your soul is black dirt because you are a Sheikh while mine is made of white and gold feathers because I am a Syed. I am militant, brash and *bad-zat* in a metal brassiere. I would gladly punch Nadim on his fucking nose. I'll get Qadir Suth to give me tight jeans and a pair of high heels, and I'll saunter through the streets of Anantnag in them.

I beg you to send your father to talk to Baba as soon as possible. Mama is on our side anyway because I have made it abundantly clear to her that I cannot live without you. However, if you choose to shut the window and sit inside, churning the esoteric rosary that Baba has assigned you to memorize and learn, nothing is going to happen. I swear by that very holy book of the Qur'an that, if need be, I'll put the entire strip of sedatives into their dinner. That will create the perfect conditions for our departure, my Sheikh, away from this house of Syeds. They will awaken with horror and stupefaction to our absence the next morning from the deep, blue haze of their drug-induced sleep.

6
Summer of 2010

~

That afternoon, Nagin had gone to buy the medicine from the pharmacy. As soon as she heard the first gunshot, she crouched on the floor behind the wooden counter. Then the bullets came flying and hit the rear wall, smashing and knocking down the glass bottles filled with a dark syrup that lined the shelves; the bullets tore through the wooden planks of the shelves and the bricks behind her. Transfixed, she heard the tramp of the soldiers' boots and the local people stampeding in terror. Her sick husband lay resting in their small, modest house, which could be reached by the narrow winding dust road leading from the marketplace on the highway to the eastern end of the town of Pampore. She was a middle-aged woman with slow gestures and a calm beauty. As a wife, she had an acute sense of duty. But she felt unlucky that day; she thought she wouldn't survive the skirmish. She was worried for her life and also worried that there would be no one to take care of Rahman if she was shot.

Amidst this clamour for freedom, *aazadi*, with the boys in the street stomping on the ground and chanting '*Go India go back, go India go back*' as they heckled and pelted the gun-toting, trigger-happy soldiers, the compounder, Inam, Sajeh's fearless son, pulled the shutter down and lay down beside the customer on the floor. Inam was still, but vigilant. Nagin's breath rasped in terror. As the noise receded with the demonstration drawing further away, Inam lit a match and whispered that there was a backdoor through which he could let her out. He motioned to her to keep her head down. The soldiers could still be waiting outside to shoot on sight.

As the two made their escape, Inam led her through the graveyard and into the long corridor of land in front of the mosque. Then he ran in the direction of the road from where they could hear screaming.

When Nagin reached home, she found her husband on the veranda.

'The gunshots woke me up and I got worried,' he quavered. His face was pale, and his hands were shaking. 'What happened in the market?'

She had a bad feeling, but she did not know the details yet.

'Something happened there,' she said casually and took him inside into the sitting room, *baithak*. She shook out the quilt and folded it neatly and made him lie down on the mattress. Then she gave him two paracetamols from the strip she had in her pocket and asked him to rest.

She spent the rest of the day cooking inside the kitchen. As night began to fall, her husband fell asleep, and she came out on the veranda. She rested her tired back against a cushion and wondered where Inam had gone. Her house shared the courtyard with Sajeh's house. She had told her what had happened earlier in the day but now she somehow felt irresponsible; had she not been frightened witless, she would have forced Inam to come home with her. She looked westward to the point where the road twisted. Beyond the cluster of tall houses, in the falling dark, she saw the angular silhouettes of the roofs go black.

After a while, Inam returned. Sajeh came out of the kitchen and confronted him in the corridor.

'Where the hell have you been? How many bullets have you taken to your chest?' Sajeh expostulated as she held him in a tight embrace. Inam was silent for a moment, perhaps remorseful too, for being careless and not returning home to his mother immediately.

But as he started talking, he became incensed. Nagin overheard him tell his mother that four boys who belonged to the households across the highway, and whom he knew very well and played cricket with occasionally, had been hit with bullets in their heads or thereabouts and three of them had died on the spot. The one who was rushed to Srinagar, the evening news bulletin on Radio Kashmir a few minutes later announced, had died in the hospital.

ॐ

One cold night, in December of 1991, Nagin was asleep on Rahman's arm in the baithak. Before dawn, Rahman woke up and went into the kitchen. He lit the lantern on the windowsill and returned to sit on the bed by her side.

'It is time to go to the shop,' he bent to whisper in her ear.

She rolled over but did not open her eyes. As she heard him get ready to leave without her, she reached out and yanked him back to the bed and pressed his head to her breast.

'I'll be late,' he groaned but she muffled his protests against her, running her fingers over his hairy shoulders. He was a huge, stout man, and she liked to feel his large, woodcutter's biceps. He squeezed her and tickled her waist. He made her giggle and coaxed her out of bed.

Down the dust track they walked together, through the faint mist of the morning. He strode purposefully, swinging the axe from one hand and holding a log of mulberry wood over his shoulder with the other. She held a lantern. They walked past clusters of houses and quietly sleeping dogs, huddled together. On either side of the road, in the gaps between the houses, the lantern's light flashed on little stretches of fields. The saffron was in bloom and the flowers gleamed in the yellow light.

When they reached the market square, it felt eerily empty and vaguely ominous. In front of their shop, one in a long row of shuttered shops flanking the highway, Rahman stood the thick, cylindrical log on the curb of the highway. As he raised his axe above his head, he swiftly scanned the area.

The army convoy started early in the morning and carried on for an hour or so. The soldiers did not stop usually, but when they did halt to let their dogs loose to sniff out landmines, they stopped the civilians and asked questions.

However, on this day, only three white jeeps hurtled through the market at a frightening speed.

Although the highway was clear, Rahman seemed distracted. He raised his axe and brought it down with a crushing blow and the log wobbled and fell down. Nagin smiled at him as she helped him to raise the log and brought the lantern closer. He glanced at her, aiming with the tip of his axe at the thin groove.

'Say *bismillah* … it won't topple over then,' Nagin said.

He smiled, gripping the handle of the axe. Then with firm control, he brought down the edge of the axe right into the groove. The log split with a loud crack into two pieces. Nagin would have clapped had Ali Mohammad not started the call for prayer.

Inside the shop with smoke-blackened, mud walls, she sat by the flat, wooden table beside the *tandoor,* oven, at the far end. On the table was a round, aluminium pan with a mound of dough. Rahman had added yeast to the atta and had left it to leaven overnight. He sprayed kerosene from the lantern over the wood chips and threw a match into the tandoor. Plumes of acrid smoke rose as the initial flames flared. She tore away at the mound, making little white spheres with her palms. Then she dusted each sphere in a bowl of dry flour.

With a quick flourish, Rahman slapped the pad against the inner wall of the tandoor, which blazed purple and blue. The first *lawas* formed, blooming with bubbles, and the delicious aroma of burnt wheat spread through the shop.

Ali Mohammad and Dr Mushtaq greeted Rahman and Nagin by their bakery door, their eyes squinting and their heads thrown back to keep away from the smoke spiralling out of the door.

Both men were in their mid-fifties. Ali Mohammad had a round face with a long white beard and large, luminous eyes. He had six daughters and only three of them had been married off. He had not done well as a contractor and in the failed deals, he had incurred debts from his friends. However, because of his clean conduct and steadfastness, his friends did not badger him for repayment. 'He'll redeem his debts when God sends him enough,' they said.

'What do I do, Dr Mushtaq?' Ali Mohammad asked, lacking his customary calm.

'You'll have to have the stamp of a gazetted officer on your identity card,' said Dr Mushtaq. 'Come to my clinic in Srinagar later today and I'll stamp it for you.'

Unlike Ali Mohammad, Dr Mushtaq never wore a pheran. He had wrapped himself in a shawl and was wearing a thick woollen sweater that reached his knees. He had a florid countenance, a high-bridged nose. He hid his bald and shiny head with a black woollen *karakul* hat.

'I want my lawas crisp,' Dr Mushtaq said to Rahman. 'And instead of eight, give me ten today; we have guests.'

'Ali Mohammad, how many do you want?' Rahman asked.

'Nagin, how is your back ache now?' Dr Mushtaq asked.

'Give me six and no more,' Ali Mohammad replied.

'The pain went away, doctor,' she replied. 'I'm feeling better.'

'Are you all right? You seem perturbed,' Rahman asked Ali Mohammad.

'Keep drinking the syrup. You'll be fine,' Dr Mushtaq said to Nagin, pulling his shawl over his shoulder. He glanced at Ali Mohammad.

'What to do?' Ali Mohammad remarked cynically. 'We live in a different time now. It is all the same … whether we live or die, what difference does it make?'

'What happened?' Rahman asked.

He put the skewer aside, uncaring that the lawas in the tandoor would burn, and stared at the two men. They stood in silence outside the door. The day had broken but the sky was covered in a dark swirl of clouds and the flickering flames caught their faces in a purple-reddish light.

'The other day the soldiers stopped Ali Mohammad,' Dr Mushtaq said. 'And because the picture he had pasted onto his identity card did not have a stamp, they slapped him.'

There was a silence. The shop filled with the gloom of humiliation. Ali Mohammad's face flushed and he bit his quivering lower lip. Before he could say anything, Nagin stood up and gathered the hot lawas from the table.

'Did you say six?' she asked, although she knew exactly how many he wanted.

'Yes, and one soft one for my Bity,' he said. Bity was his little girl.

She felt the lawas with her fingertips and found a softer one for Bity and crisp ones for Dr Mushtaq.

As soon as the two paid and were gone, Nagin told Rahman, 'I'm going, home now to cook. But before the soldiers stop you, you too must have your identity cards stamped.'

છ

Nagin stood by the window that was cluttered and gnarled with the branches of the old elm tree. The thick screen of leaves blocked out the morning sun mounting the back of the bald hill. The dark pervading the kitchen was penetrated by a single ray of light that had pierced the natural curtain like a thin needle of glittering steel. It will perforate the mud wall, it will singe my skin, Nagin thought, if I cross it, it will slash my eyes and tear a hole in my head.

It was still early in the morning and quiet inside the house. Only the ray of light roared. She glanced away from it, across the mosquito net strung over the knee-high wooden wall, towards the baithak. There Rahman lay on a mattress on the floor, under a light, darned quilt. His face had faded and his hair fell in a tangle over his eyes. He had been sleeping in the same position for a few hours now. Facing the ceiling, his lips dry and chapped, his mouth half-open. Had his chest not been faintly rising and falling, she would have thought him a dead man. Dead.

Although several weeks had passed, she recalled a moment in the shop. How prolonged that moment felt. So close to death she had been, a mere width of a needle apart. Her throat had parched and, unable to breathe, she had almost choked. That moment had been seared indelibly into her mind. Ever since then, the tiniest sounds amplified deafeningly inside her head: the buzz of a bee caught in the window netting intensified to intolerable decibels, birdcalls became raucous and agonizing. Her mood had altered as well. This morning, she was swamped by a profound bleakness. The mood within merged with the mood without because of the curfew that had been imposed as soon as the news and the heavy odour of death had spread through Pampore and all 5000 residents had resolved to give the boys a dignified funeral. She did not know the boys, but she knew Inam. Inam, a tall, tough kid who could take anything but humiliation. Since his father, Nabir, could not support his education, he had started working in Dr Mushtaq's pharmacy as soon as he matriculated, at the age of seventeen, two years ago. He knew how to give injections and he took the needle out of the flesh with such ease and confidence that it was completely painless. He was into mobile phones and girls. He had a couple of expensive black Motorola phones with English-song dial tones and the pictures of cricketers. He texted and talked to Bity during the night on the phone. He smoked cigarettes. When he had seen Nagin coming towards the shop that day, he had quickly pressed the burning end of the cigarette and stubbed it out against the counter. Not merely because he was afraid of Nagin who would report his activity to his mother, but also because he respected her. He coughed as he briskly waved away the smoke suspended in the air.

Nagin wondered about the boys: did they look like Inam when they were alive? Dressed in tight blue jeans

torn at the knees and a white T-shirt with the picture
of a blond American actor she did not know? Did they
also spike their hair with hard gel that made their gaunt
faces look gaunter? Were they still at the tender age when
colourful pimples bloomed with a soft stubble along the
innocent curve of the jaw? She had probably seen them in
the marketplace. Rahman was probably familiar with the
boys' fathers because most of Pampore came to his bakery
for bread. She had not told him what had happened. She
was afraid of what would happen if Rahman were to come
to know of the incident. She wondered what the mothers of
the boys were doing now. These boys, who had been erased
from the face of this earth, were only sixteen, thirteen and
eighteen years of age. She pictured the prayer before the
funeral. Males standing in taut lines within the compound
and women with their scarves covering their woeful, tear-
streaked faces, standing at the fringes in the surrounding
saffron fields. But the funeral had to be cancelled because
the soldiers had coerced the imam, Ali Mohammad, to
make an announcement on the mosque's loudspeaker: *If
more than three people are seen walking together anywhere,
we'll shoot them.* Inam told her that before the bodies rotted,
they should be taken elsewhere and buried. That very night
they were smuggled into a neighbouring village where they
were buried quietly.

She touched the pillow under Rahman's head with her
fingertips, leaning over him. She wanted to kiss him on
the forehead but felt that the touch of her lips would wake
him from his fitful slumber. She gently brushed his hair to

a side, listening to him breathe. The sound was distant and reassuring. He was adrift in some remote sea of sleep.

She smiled and as she stood up to go back to the kitchen, she smelled turd. It was coming from the corridor. She walked out, and realizing what had happened, she stepped through the front door and grabbed the neck of Sajeh's goat and slapped its mouth. The goat bleated, squirming from her grip.

'Damn her,' Sajeh cried, emerging from her house. In the bright sunlight, the two women surveyed the new bed of *hakh* plants that they had raised together, now laid to waste with half-nibbled green leaves.

Sajeh was a short, bright-eyed fiery woman. She moved with a great agility and ran after the goat and grabbed it by the neck.

'Keep that little beast tethered somewhere,' Nagin recommended.

Sajeh pulled at the ears of the goat and threatened, 'I'll feed you to jackals.' Then she asked Nagin in a softer voice, 'How is Rahman feeling?'

'He's burning up with fever,' Nagin said angrily. 'The pills Inam gave me are dust.'

'God be merciful. Someone has cast an evil eye on him, I am sure.'

'I don't understand the cause of his affliction.'

'God's ways. Ever since he stopped going to his bakery, I crave the saffron flavour of his flatbread, *shirmals*.'

Nagin's face softened. She nodded and smiled at Sajeh, her mind filling with the bright rose-coloured hue of her husband's face as he toiled over the hot ovens. Then, flooded with the memory of his pallor, she said, 'Even Dr Mushtaq cannot divine the cause of his disease. He says that the fever never killed anyone and Rahman will be all right, but I'm not satisfied. What I want to do though is to go to Mukhdim Sehbun in Srinagar and tie a wish-knot at the shrine. But damn this curfew! I cannot go although it's only a few miles away. There are so many soldiers on the highway that even a fly would not dare flutter its wings.'

The goat bleated again and struggled to break free of Sajeh's grip. Sajeh yanked at its ears and twisted the goat around and placed its head between her knees.

'Shut up or I'll feed you to dogs,' she scolded the goat. 'Can't you see that two women are talking?'

'We mustn't become the cause of her death,' Nagin said and they laughed. The joke was once that two woman began gossiping. The conversation stretched so long that the calf whose head one of them held between her knees was strangled to death.

'She'll be fine,' Sajeh said ironically. 'What was I telling you … Yes, the last time I went to Mukhdim Sehbun with Nabir, I saw a seer. What can I say, Nagin, about this man's piety! He must have been ninety years old, but he had such bright, angelic eyes. All he wore was a tattered pheran. When I came out of the shrine, he spotted me and stopped me on the steps. He told me he knew that I was coming out, and calling me his daughter, put a clod of clay in my hand. He told me to break it and mix with it with food if anything troubled me.'

'Did it work?' Nagin asked curiously.

'Do you remember a few days ago the boys defied curfew and pelted the soldiers on the highway? When the soldiers chased them away, the boys disappeared into the town. The soldiers were furious and they beat up Nabir who had set up his shop in the compound of the mosque, away from the highway. Nabir ran from the soldiers, abandoning his cart and crates of fruit. He came home completely out of breath, with a small wound on his forearm that bled profusely. For a moment, I was so angry that I cursed the boys. These little shits! They become so restless sitting caged inside their houses until they cannot take it anymore and they duck out. I keep Inam locked inside the room.'

'I am worried about him,' Nagin said. 'That day after walking me out of the shop, he left me in the compound of the mosque and told me to head home. I was about to ask him where he wanted to go, but he went away so quickly that I did not get a chance.'

'I said to him, "Swear on your mother's head that you won't go near the highway or touch a stone!" These young boys, they don't seem to understand that the soldiers don't care what they are beating or shooting at. Our flesh is just like wood for them ... What was I telling you? Yes, about Nabir. As the evening fell, he wanted to go back and bring his cart home, but I did not allow him to go out. He told me that it would be a major loss for us because he had invested an entire month's earnings in the cherries and apricots which he had hurriedly stashed inside the belly of the cart. But I was adamant that he stay at home. He went there the next morning and all he found was pieces of wood on the ground – not even a single box of fruit, cherries and apricots; it was all gone. When he returned home, he was so upset that he was ready to pick a fight with me.'

'What did you do then?'

'I told him not to worry. I told him about the money I had made from selling the milk of this goat,' she said, moving her knees apart a little and stroking the goat's head.

'She is still alive,' Sajeh said and Nagin laughed. 'I gave him all the money then. Although he was relieved, I could see a strange terror lurking in his eyes. It remained there all day and all evening. It felt like he had returned from a graveyard full of vicious spirits. He was silent and lost. From time to time, he burst into tears of rage. I thought he would do something dangerous, either bang his head against the kitchen wall or join the band of boys and stone the soldiers. So I put a little bit of the clay in his food. Afterwards, he slept well and was alright.'

☙

At noon, Rahman returned with a wad of cash and a bag of oranges. Together they ate lunch – the beans and rice that she had cooked. Rahman peeled the orange and gave it to her. She took the segments apart, carefully removed the fibres and gave it to him. They ate the orange segment by segment, spitting seeds on to the dasterkhwan. It was sweet, she thought.

Outside it became cloudier and she felt languorous because of the warmth induced by the food. She lay down on the mattress that she had abandoned in the morning and he followed her. He was pressed up behind her and the bed warmed up. She slipped off her pheran and he cupped her breast and caressed it. She stroked his forearms and felt him stiffen between her buttocks. She turned towards him and kissed him on his mouth. She asked him to undo the knot of her drawstring and as he did, she pulled her shalwar down. She undid his drawstring and took his penis in her hand.

When they were finished, she slipped into her pheran and went to the kitchen to drink water. As she dipped the glass into the pitcher, she glanced out of the window. It had begun to snow. The gold earring in her left ear had come loose. She gripped the hook and pushed it back into the piercing in her earlobe. She turned, smiling at Rahman lying sated on the mattress. The snowflakes twirling in joy fell on the bare brow of the hill.

ॐ

The summer deepened and the silence around her deepened. Rahman's temperature rose higher, burning his body. His condition was worsening day by day. He stopped eating altogether. He had shed weight and seemed to have shrunk further. At night, when she changed his shirt, she could feel his ribs. He had chills and he perspired profusely. In the hours before dawn, his sleep was very disturbed and he mumbled such strange things that, had it not been a question of propriety, Nagin would have grabbed the broom from the kitchen and hit the evil jinn that she suspected had possessed her husband.

At the end of a long day in mid-July, hot and exhausted, she came out of the house and sat on the veranda. She looked westward, beyond the twist in the road, at the soaring roofs of the houses. A strange restlessness overcame her, as though the gloaming contained an invisible demon of weight swelling inside her. It was then that Ali Mohammad began to give the *azan*. His voice had always been a smooth stream. But of late, as the curfew continued, it had begun to quaver. The soothing, graceful notes were missing and the recital sounded cracked and raspy.

Nagin heard a heavy jeep emerge from the bend in the road and stop at the house and saw the dark figures alighting and advancing towards the courtyard. They walked aggressively and from their arms hung tinkling handcuffs.

She went into the baithak quickly and peeping between the curtains, peered through the glass pane of the window. Although it was darker now, she could not be mistaken that the shadows were of policemen.

An icy fear crawled up her skin. She could feel gooseflesh. She recalled Sajeh saying that Inam had been missing for a day. The boys had rebelled against the curfew again and had burst on to the highway to pelt the soldiers and policemen. Inam had escaped from his room through the rear window and had joined them. Nagin realized then what was going to happen.

She quickly ran into the kitchen, lit the lantern and came back out into the courtyard.

'If you have to hit someone, hit me,' Inam shouted, 'but please don't do it in front of my parents.'

The policeman thwacked the top of his head. Nabir wept as other policemen clamped the manacles around Inam's wrists.

'They are beating, Inam! These animals are beating my son!' Sajeh shouted to alert the neighbours, hoping that a mob would arrive to overpower the armed forces.

'Please don't,' Nabir begged the policemen.

Nagin was only a few feet away from them, standing at the entrance door. The policeman quickly encircled Inam and marched him to the jeep.

Nagin ran to Nabir who was slapping his forehead and beating his chest. 'They are taking him away,' he wailed.

'What's the point of crying?' Sajeh asked. 'Do something, Nabir!'

'What do you want me do?' Nabir asked.

'Nothing,' Sajeh said. 'Nagin, take him inside. I'll go to Ali Mohammad and Dr Mushtaq and tell them that they took my son away.'

'Are they going to beat him up?' Nabir asked.

'Shut up,' Sajeh said. 'Do me a favour, Nagin, take him into the house and give him a glass of water.'

When Sajeh returned, she said, 'Dr Mushtaq asked us to wait for a day. He said he would have called a police officer he knows, but the mobile service has been suspended. I'll go tomorrow and take Dr Mushtaq and Ali Mohammad with me and find this police officer.' Nabir sighed but did not say anything. Nagin nodded at Sajeh and stood up.

'You should go,' Sajeh said. 'Rahman must be waiting for you.'

Rahman was sitting up against the wall in the baithak. His eyes were scrunched and he was biting his dry burning lips.

Nagin, entering the kitchen, quickly stepped over the low partition wall and went to him. She inserted a pillow behind his back. He gave off a strong sickly odour. And though he looked at her, he did not seem to recognize her.

'I am here, Rahman,' she said softly and wiped the corners of his lips with the edge of her scarf. 'You have not eaten anything for the last twenty-four hours.' She went back to the kitchen and warmed a cup of salt tea and put an old *tschevor* in it. She also added a pinch of clay that Sajeh had given her and brought it to him on a tray.

After she fed him a few spoonfuls, his eyes opened. But then he closed his mouth. 'I'm not hungry. I feel drowsy and nauseous,' he said.

'You have to tell me what you feel exactly,' Nagin was surprised to discover anger in her tone.

'I feel weak in my body and sick in my heart.'

'You have no disease, do you know that? Dr Mushtaq says you have no disease.'

'I want to go to my shop.'

'You'll go to your shop as soon as the curfew ends.'

'The police took away Inam. Why did they take him away?'

'God will protect him,' she said. 'Mukhdim Saeb will protect him.'

'What if they do something to him?' He forestalled her attempt to interrupt him. 'What if they beat him to death in prison?' he asked.

'Stop saying such ominous things. He'll return home and you'll go back to your shop.'

'I will die of this illness, Nagin. Like these boys who throw stones at the soldiers and get shot, I'll die this summer.'

'I beg of you, please don't say things like this,' she pleaded.

'I know him well and I know what kind of boy he is. If they release him, he will join his friends on the streets and stone the soldiers. If he survives this madness, I want him to come and stay with us. I want him to help me burn a load of firewood and prepare a clean and warm tandoor. We'll knead dough and make shirmals. So many shirmals we will make, Nagin; and we will sprinkle each shirmal with poppy seeds. We'll make shirmals for all of Pampore—' He broke off as tears filled his eyes.

'Go back to sleep now, my dear, and you'll have this later.' She put the cup back on the tray.

'I'm afraid of sleep. Why don't you lie down with me?' Rahman asked. 'When I fall asleep, I feel I'm falling through darkness.'

She nodded, moved the quilt to the side and sat on the mattress close to him.

'In the middle of the night, my heart suddenly starts thumping,' he said, putting his head on her lap. 'If you aren't in bed by my side, I will die in that moment.'

She hugged him. 'Why won't I be there?'

'I am so afraid of being lonely in the moments before death, Nagin,' he said.

'Hush now, don't say anything,' she said, and put her hand comfortingly around the nape of his neck. She moved his head back to the pillow and lay down beside him. 'Put your arm down for me,' she said.

'As long as I live, it is your pillow,' he said and chuckled.

7
The Miscreant

～

On the third day of their captivity, Mohsin found himself sitting beside Tariq, their bare backs against a stone wall. The cell that they were brought into at noon smelt pungently of blood, urine and excrement, its thick stone walls muffling the echoes of wails and shrieks from neighbouring cells. The only exit to the outside world was a heavy door with iron bars on the opposite wall, which led through the dimly lit hallway to the Tunnel.

Mohsin's left hand was handcuffed to Tariq's right. The food that followed the beatings and starvation animated them and Tariq burst into tears. Suddenly, struck by a thought, he stopped sobbing and said, 'Imagine God being subjected to our pain.'

Mohsin rebuked him sharply for even thinking such a terrible thing and warned him that they were no longer on the ledge beneath the bridge to gather rocks from the bed of the stream and discuss strategies to pelt Force 10 as he passed by in his cavalcade of jeeps through the marketplace. They were in a damn prison where they might be beaten to death; Tariq shouldn't start his philosophy lecture there and talk drivel.

'You're a fucking coward,' Tariq hissed back.

Mohsin yanked the manacle and Tariq yelped and shouted, 'What the hell do you think you're doing?'

Mohsin turned away, his face filled with loathing. He wanted to yank at Tariq's wrist again and break away from him – his vile, noxious friend.

'Why, then,' Mohsin asked in a perplexed tone, 'did you come out of your house? Was it only to throw stones at the police?'

'I am troubled by my memory, Mohsin,' said Tariq in a quiet voice. 'I ran into a soldier six years ago, during the summer that I turned eighteen. On returning home after my fateful encounter with him, I joined Father and Mother for lunch, and put the memory of the two pigeons that he had made me kill out of my mind. Later that day, I retired to my bedroom on the third floor – ours is an ancient house, you know. Every time I went inside, no matter how much I used the broom and rag, the grime on the wooden floor and the withering wooden walls would return. Over a period of time, I grew used to it: the sandy, brown stuff smelling of mould and lassitude.

'The sun was above the Wall in the west and when I went into my bedroom after lunch, I began to feel drowsy. I shut the windows, drew the curtains and lay on my bed which was right up against the window. I put a pillow under my head and picked up the remote control from the windowsill and switched on the TV. It was time for *Upheavals,* a documentary series on the History Channel about Latin America that I followed religiously.

'I was deep in a scorching, brown desert on the border between Mexico and Texas when an unexpected gust of wind pushed the window open, the shutter knocked against my arm, and I dropped the remote control. The string that held the curtain snapped and like an unfurling flag, the curtain flew across the room. Through the window I watched as the sudden storm raged across Srinagar and shook the Wall. The stream that passed by it had finally lost its stagnant stupor and was swelling, swirling and flowing. And then the two pigeons entered. I quickly pushed the window shut; I wanted to capture them. But the pigeons had turned into stupendous metallic creatures. Their eyes were red, their beaks sharp, and their wings gleaming. If they bite me, I'll bleed to death, I thought. They circled overhead, their wings like little swords; they tore against the sheets of still air inside, causing the eternal grime from the floor to rise. They flew in tangents, grazing and bruising the walls, until they landed on top of the TV. The pigeons pecked frenziedly on the screen behind which a mutiny was going on. They, the pigeons, terrified the gun-toting gringos on horseback and the Mexican rebels cheered. The spectacle continued until the horses whinnied, their hoofs trampled and a slaughter began. In their mad fury the pair of pigeons attacked the screen with their beaks, their hoary feathers swirling and floating before me. My head clanged inside and I felt giddy, as if the pigeons were circling not in my bedroom but inside my head. I watched this drama as though in a bizarre dream with breathless astonishment until the birds escaped through the window that the violent wind had banged open again.

'As soon as they left, the rebels fell and mingled with the dust on the ground and the storm abated. I lit a cigarette and stood by the window. The Wall was erect and the waters in the stream were still and as muddy as ever. As the sun sank behind it, the sky turned a dull purple hue and copper clouds moved into the middle over the Wall. My room was deserted and the pigeons were gone as though they had never existed, as though beyond the Wall that blocked my vision of Srinagar and the last glimpses of that day's sun, they were dead – eternally dead. Although I was sad, I didn't feel wracked with guilt. I never was guilt-ridden. What was there to be guilty about as long as one lived and longed?

'I remember on that day I had walked out of my house for the shrine where you and Father go to pray these days – where both of you fool yourselves that the dead saint is alive and that you are earthly vassals of some divine god. Ha, ha! What dogmatic fools you are, to be sure! Faith, my friend, is the consolation of the weak and foolish. It's only good for those who can afford it, whose quest for life and curiosity to contemplate reality it can douse with the promise of a halo of light. But not for those whose feet are planted firmly on the ground, not for those who are not blind to the veins cut open by time, and not for those who are tuned to the History

Channel and watch and reflect on the human waste and the
scale of human cruelty. Imagine the mounds of dead bodies
in the sand. Imagine the mosaics of blood on the wall. Inhale
the stink of your shame, Mohsin.

'I am older than you, by five years. I left home early and
made solitary excursions beyond the Himalayas into the
world. I was ambitious. I wanted to commit to memory all of
Will Durant's thick tomes by the time I turned twenty-five.
I wanted to understand the history of human beings – that
is essentially the history of human cruelty. I wanted to know
what drove the king of Akkad, Sargon the Great, to Assyria,
I wanted to know what brought the Indian soldiers from the
Gangetic plain to the city of Srinagar during the notorious
October in 1947.

'My father must have told you what followed, the
extravagant story of my failure. You must have heard that
I was rusticated from the schools in New Delhi and the
schools in Islamabad. I had my stance and I stood by it, no
matter what. I got into heated debates until I became so
fervid and eloquent that my counterparts felt I was insulting
them. I was expelled from these damned cities and, hell yeah,
it gave me immense pleasure. Truth be told, over the past
many years, it has deepened in me the sense of who I am – a
Kashmiri and nothing else.

'I'm impudent and cheeky. That's my gift and my curse.
As Father must have told you as you two joined hands in
blind faith inside the mosque, I fart from my mouth. People
find my words nasty and blasphemous. But, inside me, every
night when I return to my bedroom, sniffing at the grime, I

feel a longing as though my heart is a dry stone craving water. A feeling akin to what I had felt for a fleeting moment as I looked at the gilded words of the Qur'an on the shroud over the saint's grave. I had leaned to gather the dead bodies of the pigeons by my feet, the pigeons – their eyes wide open and pleading – that I had felled with a single bullet of the soldier's gun. I articulate what I believe in, and I believe in what I articulate. War is as real as death. And I shall not pretend, Mohsin, I am done with keeping my face and acting as though all is hunky-dory, as though they ever were hunky-dory: my dear, I am terrified of death.

'What was I telling you? Yes, after the pigeons left, I stood by the window watching the sun disappear behind the Wall and the darkness fall. I stood there brooding in the stagnant dusk. I longed for something dramatic and extreme. I longed for death and I wanted to kill someone. I was so frustrated, I wanted to go inside the bathroom and cut myself until I began to bleed. I wanted to jump out through the window into the kitchen garden which was already in shambles. I wanted to throw a stone at the Wall. I should have seized the frightening bliss of that moment; I should have dived headlong into the muddy stream.

'Mohsin, my dear friend, you are exactly like me, fortuitous and frail. I know you think I am crazy in my head. But trust me, one rarely achieves originality and splendour in one's life except in the moment like the one I experienced right after the pigeons left me. One goes on living and looking at the Wall. One is not spared the pain and defeat and degradation. One is not spared the silent horrors of boredom and banality.

But had I seized that moment, I'd have been spared the ordeal of living in this dungeon, and the curse of living in the besieged city of Srinagar at the beginning of the twenty-first century.

'Mohsin, you look dubious. You probably think that I've lost my sanity with the beatings that Force 10 gave us. Allow me to explain. I know you think I am completely wrong in my conception of the world and after-world. The only thing I cannot accept is your claim that you're unafraid of death because you are. And you think if Force 10 kills you, you'll become a martyr and live eternally in a world that is just and lasting. Bullshit. What kind of fool's paradise are you living in? And how dare you think of paradise when Kashmir still exists on earth. Why the fuck don't you understand that the occupation itself is the deepest circle of hell and there is no hell beyond it? Remember one thing: men and women are merely men and women, and whenever and wherever they are shackled, their movement curtailed and their freedom taken away, they will rebel and launch a hailstorm—'

The door opened at that moment and interrupted Tariq's rant. Force 10 moved towards them in the semi-dark, the keys clinking in his hand. He directed the light of his torch at their faces, piercing their eyes with the sharp beam of light. Then he grabbed the manacle that shackled the boys together and unlocked it.

'If you move or open your mouth, I will drill holes in your head,' he warned them and dragged Tariq to the door and tied him to the bar in the centre. Then he came back to Mohsin and said, 'Follow me.'

In the hallway, Mohsin saw Force 10 more clearly. Dressed in khaki overalls and lumberjack shoes, he had marked his forehead with three lines of charcoal. Mohsin gave him a sharp sideways glance, recalling how Force 10's mouth had frothed when he had beaten him with his belt. Force 10's determination to break Mohsin's body was so strong that each blow he delivered was harder than the one that preceded it. As they approached the washbasin fitted into the wall to their right, Force 10 halted.

'Put that shirt on,' he said, gesturing to the side of the mirror tacked onto the wall. A white, long-tailed shirt, without any spots of blood, hung from a nail.

Mohsin put it on and stood before the mirror, looking at the bottom of the washbasin which contained broken teeth, saliva and blood.

'Wash your fucking face,' Force 10 said.

Mohsin obeyed, but with his eyes shut, unable to look at himself after three days of torture and relentless beatings. He did not want to see the defeat in his eyes and a broken body covered with innumerable gashes. He glanced away from his reflection and looked at Force 10 who gestured to him to walk to the Tunnel.

Past Café Barbarica, Force 10 opened a door to his right and pushed Mohsin into the office that was suffused with sunlight. The walls were washed white and supported a high-vaulted ceiling.

'Stand there in the middle,' Force 10 ordered Mohsin and walked out through the front door.

Inspector Masoodi was seated behind the table, resting his arms on the soft arms of a leather chair. Rumour had it that Masoodi believed in the same God that Mohsin did, the God about whom Tariq was sceptical. About Inspector Masoodi it was said that wherever he was posted in Kashmir, he built an opulent mosque where he prayed five times a day from the front row. He was a clean, uniformed man with a florid face and a thick, groomed moustache. With his black baton, he tapped the wooden table top, and Force 10 entered with Mohsin's mother.

'Inspector Sahib, please let Mohsin go,' she pleaded in tears.

'Sit down and be silent,' Inspector Masoodi commanded, pointing to the chair across him.

As she sat down, she glanced at Mohsin's swollen and bruised countenance. 'What has become of you, my son,' she choked.

Inspector Masoodi gazed coldly at Mohsin. He placed his baton on the table and folding his arms across his chest, he sat back in his chair.

'Your son is a miscreant,' he said to the weeping woman. 'He has strayed from the path that God ordained for us in the Qur'an.'

'Is it I who has strayed?' Mohsin shouted indignantly. He could scarcely believe what he was hearing. He felt the pain of the beating seeping into every inch of his body.

'Mohsin, shut up,' his mother said.

'You can see for yourself that this kid has no manners,' Inspector Masoodi said. 'It's all the same – he who breaks the law of the land, breaks the law of God.'

'He's innocent,' the woman protested.

'He is a miscreant,' Inspector Masoodi said.

'I beg of you, please let him go.'

'I will let him go if he recites from the Qur'an,' Inspector Masoodi said, leaning forward, his elbows on the table. 'I will let him go if he recites the chapter, *Al Fatiha*, the line: *Guide us on the straight path*.'

'Mohsin, please do whatever he says,' his mother begged him.

'Do you honestly expect me to recite the Qur'an in front of this man?' Mohsin asked, incredulous. 'Does he even know how perverse he is?'

'Do whatever he says, Mohsin,' his mother repeated.

'Where does the recitation of the Qur'an fit into the business of custodial torture?'

'Mohsin, your mother begs you.'

'Mother, not on my life, not in front of this hypocrite,' said Mohsin.

'Then you will rot in this prison,' Inspector Masoodi said, rising. He pointed the tip of his baton towards Mohsin's chest.

'Inspector Sahib, he is innocent,' his mother wept.

'Mother, I'm anything but innocent. I throw stones at the soldiers and police. I'm a criminal and my crime is that I am besotted with the spectre of freedom. I won't stop pelting policemen like him until all of them have been driven out of Kashmir.'

'Inspector Sahib, please forgive him, he doesn't know what he's saying,' she entreated, pressing her palms together and bowing towards the policeman.

'Silence!' Inspector Masoodi shouted furiously, striking the table with the baton. Force 10, standing in the lawns, came in running. 'Take this woman away and throw this boy back into the cell.'

ৎ

As Force 10 led Mohsin back through the Tunnel into the hallway, they could hear Tariq singing:

Bring me back my moment,
bring me back my pair of pigeons.

My friend has gone mad, Mohsin rued in his heart. Who could possibly remain sane in this theatre of cruelty? As he walked in through the door, his eyes met Tariq's and there was a moment of acknowledgement. Mohsin wanted to tell Tariq, 'I don't believe in Inspector Masoodi's God. His God is very different from mine.'

As they approached the washbasin, Force 10 asked Mohsin to remove the shirt. Mohsin peeled it off and hung it back on the nail. He looked into the mirror and his blood-shot eyes stared back at him. His lower lip was torn; his face was grotesquely swollen.

Force 10 stood behind him and looked on impassively. Inside the cell, Tariq continued his insane singing.

'Can I have some water?' Mohsin asked.

'Okay, but hurry up,' Force 10 replied. Mohsin was taken aback by Force 10's inexplicable lenience. He leaned over the basin and turned the faucet. Force 10 stepped away to lean against the wall behind him. He lit a cigarette and took a drag and the smell of burnt tobacco and dry weed filled the chamber.

'Stop singing that damn song,' Force 10 coughed, 'or I'll wring your neck and tear your lungs out.'

Tariq stopped singing. Force 10 dialled a number on his cell phone. Mohsin washed his face and drank a palmful of water. As he placed his hands on the sides of the washbasin, he felt it move slightly. Mohsin looked at Force 10 in the mirror. He was engrossed with the phone and had turned away. Mohsin saw the shaved nape of his neck. Wrapped in the pleasant odour of the smoke, Force 10 laughed luridly and clicked his tongue. He seemed to be talking dirty to a woman.

Mohsin grabbed the washbasin with both hands and moved it. With one swift motion, he tore it off the wall and turned, holding the ceramic basin aloft.

Force 10 fell to the floor, unconscious. His eyes were open, the blood gushing out of the wide wound in his head. There was a long silence until Tariq resumed his song.

Bring me back my moment
Bring me back my pair of pigeons.

8
The Stone Thrower

&

A tall, young car-washer in grease-smeared blue jeans and a white T-shirt was on his way home from the market. He walked straight on the dust road towards his home, looking ahead intently, across the wooden bridge with wooden railings. The house was at the end of the street, small and shoddy, with cracked clay walls and a crumbling, rust-eaten roof.

As he stepped on to the bridge, he saw his mother, squatting on the bank of the stream. Dipping the bucket in her hand into the water, she glanced up.

'I bought spinach and tomatoes,' Mohsin said matter-of-factly, slightly raising the plastic bag that he held in his hand.

'I'll get the cheese later and make you your favourite dish,' his mother said and smiled. There was pain in her eyes.

As the bucket filled with the water, it pulled at her arm. She resisted the tow, pulling the bucket up and out. Her snood, a thin, worn rag of white cotton, came loose, exposing her grey, discoloured hair. But before it could slide down to her shoulders, embarrassing her before her son and other passers-by, she grabbed hold of it. Placing the bucket on the slippery bank between her feet, she pulled the snood by its ends, wrapped it around her head and tied a secure knot. Then she picked up the bucket and stepped on to the thin strip of tall grass and reeds by the road.

Mohsin was about to offer to carry the bucket home, but she waved him to go on ahead. 'Tea is ready in the kitchen,' she said.

Mohsin nodded and was about to continue in the direction of home when he heard a noise – the hiss of a firecracker tearing through the air before hitting what sounded like a heavy sack of rice.

The bucket fell from his mother's hand and tumbled on to the broken tarmac. He turned and ran back across the bridge. His mother ran after him.

A boy, whose name turned out to be Amir, had fallen on the grass verge by the road, his face turned skyward. He wore a white school shirt and grey trousers. His skull was split. Blood and brain matter had trickled out on to his face. His satchel was flung on the tarmac, in the middle of the road. The smoke shell was by his feet amidst the notebooks and pencils that had spilled out of the satchel. A plume of acrid smoke rose from it.

Mohsin's mother gave a cry of horror. Untying the knot, she threw her snood over Amir's face. Mohsin put the plastic bag down and held her by her arm. He looked down the road in the direction of the market. There he saw Force 10, the policeman whose car he had washed once. Force 10 wore a green helmet and held a stun gun in his hand.

'Mohsin, bring water, bring water,' his mother cried. 'Let us wash this boy's face.'

Mohsin ran across the bridge and grabbed the fallen bucket by its handle. He jumped over the green strip on to the bank. As he dipped the bucket into the brook, bright bubbles emerged noisily out of the water and burst on the surface.

His mother was kneeling by Amir's head. Beneath the scarf, she glimpsed the blood trickling down Amir's jaw, gathering in the hollow of his throat between the collarbones. Unable to bear the sight of it, she wept hysterically.

Neighbours gathered around. Mohiddin held Mohsin's mother, turning her head away from the boy felled on the road. '*Ya Rasullallah, Ya Rasullallah,*' he recited. Najib fidgeted and muttered under his breath. He stepped back, rushed forward and kicked the shell with his shoe like a football player. It rolled over the edge of the bridge and fell into the stream.

As it hit the water, it exploded. The entire stream frothed violently, splashing Mohsin's face. Najib gritted his teeth and let loose a stream of profanity.

Mohsin returned with the bucket of water and asked Mohiddin to take his mother away. Then he picked up the snood from Amir's face and threw it on to the tarmac.

Amir's face was splotched with blood, his eyes clogged. Red flesh hung loosely from his forehead.

Mohsin lifted the boy's head into his lap and sprinkled a palmful of water from the bucket on his face. He rinsed his fingers in the bucket, dissolving the blood, and the white and grey matter clinging to his fingertips. He dribbled some water on to Amir's temples, washing them. 'Give me the scarf,' he said to Najib, who was standing by Amir's feet. But Najib stood motionless, gaping at the gash the shell had made in Amir's head.

'Give me the scarf, you idiot,' Mohsin snapped. Najib looked startled, as though he had been woken from a nightmare. He picked up the strip of cloth from the road and raised it like a flag. The dirt from the street clung to the wet patches of blood and brain on the snood. Najib whipped the fabric to shake off the muck before handing it to Mohsin.

The wound continued to bleed and ooze. Mohsin's mother was wailing at the bridge. Mohiddin, still holding her arm, was loudly reciting: '*Ya Rasullallah, Ya Rasullallah.*' Najib paced restlessly. He lit up a cigarette suddenly, not caring that Mohiddin, a venerable elder, whom the young men respected enough to not smoke in his presence, was in their midst.

Mohsin wound the fabric around the wound and fished out Amir's ID card and mobile phone from his trouser pocket. The cell phone's screen was broken with multiple cracks radiating across the tiny glass pane, however it lit up obligingly when Mohsin pressed the button to activate it. He scrolled to the contacts and dialled the first number on the list, *Abba.*

'Where are you, Amir?' Abba asked. Mohsin was silent. He had no words to say to the father of the boy whom he had not seen before today; a man whose son's name, age and the school he attended he had learnt after he was dead.

'Are you still at the tuition centre? Your mother was asking what was taking you so long, Amir.'

'I'm calling from—' Mohsin began.

'Who are you?' Abba interrupted. 'And why are you using Amir's phone?'

'Amir has had an accident,' Mohsin replied, not knowing what else to say.

'Is he okay? Where is he now?' Abba asked.

ॐ

Across the lake, Amir's village was at the foot of a hill. As news of Amir's death spread, the people of the neighbourhood thronged to the house. Within minutes, a casket had been organized, sheets of tarp spread over the courtyard and a tent erected at the far end beside a dense walnut coppice.

On this day, Mohsin's clothes had different stains and smears. Not the usual black smears of grease but the pale grey smears of brains. Not the yellow stains of oil, but the red stains of blood. He stood with the school satchel, holding it close to his chest. He had gathered and put Amir's pencils, notebooks, mobile phone and wallet inside it. He pressed his back to the metal grill of the veranda, fixing his eyes on the tent. Through a little gap, over the heads of wailing women with headscarves of bright, flaming colours, he watched Mohiddin raise Amir's small, pale arm and wash it.

Mohsin's hunger had vanished. A languor came over him and he felt morose and dazed. He listened listlessly to the uneven shuffle of footsteps around him. Young boys and girls shepherding in the old and weak, bringing them tumblers of cold water from inside the house, whispering consolation and condolences into their ears. Mohsin stood there looking towards the sky the sun had fogged up. The air was oppressive and still. He closed his eyes and overheard two boys.

'I had told you that Force 10 was following us everywhere. Even in the ground where we went to play cricket.'

'But Amir did not throw stones. He only wished to.'

'*We* did and Force 10 saw him playing with us later.'

'Where can the policeman hide? Next time, we'll finish him.'

'There's plenty of bricks and rocks in the streets of the city.'

Mohsin turned around and saw the two boys. They were barely fifteen or sixteen. Although they were not crying, their faces were streaked with tears, their eyes swollen and red with rage. They saw Mohsin watching them.

'He was our friend,' Nazir said.

'We were in the same class,' Imtiyaz added.

Mohsin wanted to ask them more questions about Amir, but Najib who was inside the tent, waved at him, beckoning him inside.

He moved through the narrow aisle between the women seated on the tarp sheets, and the two boys followed him. A grieving woman suddenly rose from the centre of a cluster of women to his left and pointed her finger at him. 'That satchel belongs to my son,' she cried. Her eyes were swollen and her hair was in disarray. She slapped herself on her forehead and sobbed. She seized her pheran and ripped it from the collar down to her belly. She leaped over the women seated around her and snatched the schoolbag from Mohsin. She kissed it and hugged it, still self-flagellating and intoning her son's name during the pauses. The women rose to hold the bereft mother and escorted her into the house.

Inside the tent, it was dark and still. People's faces were barely discernible and the voices themselves sounded muffled. The centre tent pole appeared too fragile to hold up the weight of the canvas and Mohsin was afraid that the entire edifice would crash down on the mourners.

Following Najib's instructions, Mohsin and the boys hefted the casket to the side. Abba wrapped Amir in a white shroud. He raised his son's upper body, holding the shoulders of the corpse, and Najib and Mohsin lifted the feet. Mohiddin raised the lid of the casket and together they lowered the dead body into it. As Mohiddin secured the lid, Abba looked him in the eye, frowning; he seemed discombobulated. What if my son woke up inside the casket? he seemed to ask. Would he not need air to breathe?

Abba gave a cry and his knees buckled. Before he could collapse, Nazir and Imtiyaz grabbed his shaking shoulders and held him upright.

A year ago, Mohiddin's son, Ishfaq, had escorted his cousin to her house after dinner, driving her in his car. On his way back home, he had passed by a military camp. The car, a mere machine, lacked the mechanism to understand the dire consequences of breaking down in a city like Srinagar. The car stalled in front of the military bastion on that dark night. The soldiers in the bunker at the end of the fence facing the road became suspicious. That is not perfectly accurate – the soldiers here were always paranoid. For them, the city was a dangerous jungle, the roads, fanged serpents feigning sleep. Any car coming to a sudden stop in front of their camp was a ploy to dynamite them. That fateful night, when the car spluttered and died, they yelled at the driver, asking him to go away. When he failed to do so, they shot him.

Later that night, when Mohiddin received his son's corpse, following the initial staggering shock, he performed the ablutions and recited from the Qur'an. He admonished his wife, son and their neighbours – Mohsin and his mother, Zarin and Najib – who had come to mourn, forbidding lamenting. The boy's chest was riddled with bullets – seventeen of them. In the ritual of final cleansing, the father had washed away the blood around the wounds. When he had shrouded the body, he embalmed it with the perfume he had bought from Medina years ago while he was on pilgrimage. He asked a few young men to help him place the body in the casket. He was the foremost pallbearer and when the procession reached the graveyard, he announced: 'I'm going to bury my son myself.'

Across the coppice, the father who still mourned the death of his own son, now led the funeral prayer in the graveyard by the shore of the lake. Mohsin stood between Najib and Abba, his hands clasped over his heart. Unlike the coppice and the backyard, the lake in the front was placid. In the thickening heat haze, the sun in the sky was a mere blood-orange blot. It hung low over the lake, making the city look surreal.

As the prayer began, Mohsin's heart heaved. He wanted to run away from the mourners, now mutely grappling with the suddenness of their loss. Abba's and Najib's shoulders were crowding him in. He longed to push them away. He wanted to catechize Mohiddin about his stoic fortitude that sustained him despite having had to witness coffin after coffin containing the corpses of children and young men. From where did he get the courage to lead the prayers? How come he hadn't suffered a nervous breakdown and gone to pieces?

In that moment, Mohsin hated him. He wanted to be like him: at peace amidst the upheavals and turbulence of war. He wanted something to hold on to as he waded through the sea of cadavers. He found it difficult to breathe. The heaviness in his chest turned to a dull ache that spread across his limbs and head. He was nauseous and thirsty. The duration of the prayer lengthened extraordinarily.

Amir's mother's wails seemed to emerge like little white birds that winged through the walnut trees into the cemetery. In Mohsin's fevered imagination, they circled over his head, dripping blood from their bruised wings.

When the prayer finally ended, the birds soared away across the lake where, blinded by the heat haze, they plummeted into the water and drowned.

ॐ

A grassy area of about fifty yards separated the main road from the concrete elevation of the garage where Mohsin worked. The cars moved slowly by the shop in the front where Najib sold magazines and newspapers; they came in along the dirt track strewn with boulders and went up the inclination on to the concrete elevation where Mohsin expertly cleaned them.

A year ago, towards the end of his first week at work, Mohsin was on the dirt track. With one eye on the road, to keep a sharp lookout for potential customers, he was chatting with Najib who was in the shop, seated in his chair behind the counter with the customary cigarette hanging from his mouth. Najib absently flicked through a magazine as he made desultory conversation with Mohsin. A Zen veered off the road and hurtled towards Mohsin. Had Mohsin not stepped back in time, he'd have been tossed over the bonnet of the car.

The Zen screeched to a halt at the elevation. The door opened and out came Force 10. He was a tall man with a thin face. His brown eyes had an unusual blue tint. He had a beaky nose and a small, rodent-like mouth.

Mohsin, who had fallen on the boulders, stood up, dusting himself. Force 10 threw the keys at him and Mohsin reflexively caught them before they hit his face.

'Have it cleaned up, kid, by the time I get back,' Force 10 said and walked across the road and into the market.

'Do you know him?' Mohsin asked Najib.

'Sick, son-of-a-bitch,' Najib replied, tossing the cigarette stub on to the track. 'He is the new SHO.'

When he returned half an hour later, Mohsin had washed the car. He handed him the keys. 'Two hundred rupees, sir,' he said.

Force 10 took the keys. Using his long, bony fingers as pincers, he gripped Mohsin's jaw and stared into his eyes menacingly. Then he slowly released him and at the last moment he slapped Mohsin.

'Do you want more?' he asked.

Mohsin just stood there stupidly, speechless as he watched Force 10 unlock the car door and get into his vehicle.

Mohiddin, who was buying a newspaper at the shop, saw the entire episode. As Force 10 started up the car, reversed it and sped away, he came over to Mohsin, as did Najib. Mohsin felt deeply humiliated by the pity and compassion in their eyes and wanted to run away and hide.

'If I could,' Najib said, 'I'd break his head with a stone.'

'Shut up, Najib,' Mohiddin said. He stroked Mohsin's head gently. 'Be patient, son. Be careful,' he added.

This is the first week of my work, Mohsin wanted to scream. What was he supposed to tell his hopeful mother who, although she never overtly mentioned it, wanted him to build a new house before he got married? That he had toiled in vain using a gallon of soap water to scrub the windows and tyres, and had dusted the filthy seats and erased the flecks of blood from the dashboard and steering wheel – what was Force 10, a cop or a fucking criminal? That he had sprayed air freshener into the interior of the car that reeked of weed, alcohol and cum – all for nothing?

'Just make an exception in his case,' Mohiddin advised Mohsin. Najib tried butting in at this point, but Mohiddin shooed him away. He took out two one-hundred-rupee notes from his wallet and tucked them into the breast pocket of Mohsin's shirt.

Mohsin lowered his eyes, blushing as grateful tears sprang to his eyes. He shook his head and returned the money.

'Foolish, boy, keep it,' rebuked Mohiddin, holding him in an embrace.

A month later, when Mohsin refused to wash Force 10's car for free again, he drove him along the rim of the lake, and jolting him in the back seat, sped past the apple orchards to pull over in front of an old colonial mansion. The walls of the mansion, built into the cliff that was covered with pines and ivy, were washed white. It had a square garden in the front with rose hedges and cherry trees. Odd as it may sound, on the door of the mansion, the sign read: POLICE STATION.

Force 10 marched him past the living room that served as the office and through a door at the back into a tunnel. The row of ceiling bulbs didn't quite dispel the gloom here and water seeped through the stone walls.

At the end of the tunnel, Force 10 shoved Mohsin into a hallway that opened into a cell with a door of iron bars. He shackled his prisoner's arm to the door and unbuckled his belt.

'You asked for payment,' he grabbed Mohsin's face with his claw-like fingers and glared into his face with bloodshot eyes. He hit Mohsin's manacled wrist repeatedly with the metal buckle. 'You ... asked *me* ... to pay *you* ... money?' he bellowed. After Force 10 had broken all the bones in Mohsin's wrist, he undid the cuffs and dragged the semi-conscious lad through the damp tunnel. He hauled him past the living room and out of the mansion and dumped his body in a rose bush.

Thirty-six hours later, when Mohsin opened his eyes, he was in bed at home. His wrist was in a cast. He saw Mohiddin and his mother standing at his bedside.

'These young boys never listen to us,' Mohiddin complained. 'Don't they realize that an entire army is out there to break their bodies?'

ॐ

She was a sad, shrivelled woman with frail arms and grainy skin. There were dark circles around her grey, misty eyes. She had aged prematurely. Barbed wrinkles ran across her temples, creating tangles of beleaguered grief. Hamid, her husband, had disappeared seventeen years ago when she was barely twenty-four years old and Mohsin, a mere toddler. She had registered numerous missing persons reports at innumerable police stations. Holding her husband's photograph, framed in glass and wood, against her chest, she had picketed in the public parks along with other women who had lost their menfolk to the unrest that had broken out in 1989. With civil rights activists and human rights lawyers, she had visited military camps to plead her case to top-ranking officers. A lascivious lawyer offered to promote her case in exchange for an extramarital affair with him. He proposed that she spent a night with him, in a hotel on the outskirts of the city. No one would know, he told her. She became angry but nevertheless thought about it; her nights were long and lonely and the desire for a man's intimate touch pulsed through her body, the memory of her husband, flooding in. She felt guilty of her thoughts for reasons she could understand and reasons she could not. She cried as she resolved to refuse the lawyer, devoting herself entirely to her son.

Mohsin was all she had. He was grown up now, the shadow of a moustache over his upper lip resembled his father's.

A few days after Amir's killing, before the spinach would shrivel and tomatoes rot, she bought a wedge of cheese from the market and cooked Mohsin his favourite dish. When Mohsin returned in the afternoon, she prettied herself up, donning a new headscarf and freshly laundered clothes. In the entranceway, he smelled the delightful aroma of garlic.

She asked him to sit in the narrow sitting room that was across the corridor from the kitchen and she brought out the festive, yellow and black printed dasterkhwan and spread it before him. But as she unfurled it on the floor, it reminded Mohsin of his mother's old snood with which he had shrouded Amir's face.

She returned with a tray on which she had placed a bowl of water, a bowl of yoghurt, a plate of white rice and a bowl of cheese dish cooked with spinach. She sat beside him, smiling and watching him eat. He kept glancing at the dasterkhwan and his mother's new snood. He suddenly stopped eating.

'Is the cheese burnt?' his mother asked anxiously. 'Haven't I cooked it the way you like it?'

'It is not that, mother,' he replied. He did not want to upset her, but a great icy weight had settled in his stomach and had killed his appetite. The image of Amir's face, his eyes glued shut by singed, swollen flesh, flashed across his mind.

'I'm full,' he said.

'But you haven't had enough,' she protested.

'I'm full, mother,' he said loudly and immediately regretted yelling at her. He rinsed his hand in the pot and, drinking a long sip of water, he rose.

'Where are you going?' she asked.

'I'll be back soon,' he said tersely. As he said these words, he was filled with an ominous premonition that he was going to share Amir's fate very soon.

He emerged from his house, an ugly monstrosity that he had failed to refurbish. He strode away from the entrance door towards the market. He was amazed that the world went on with its humdrum routines without even pausing to acknowledge Amir's death. How can I eat after Amir's skull was shattered right there on the street? he asked himself.

When he approached the bridge, he vaulted over the strip of reeds and on to the bank. He rolled up the bottom edge of his trousers to his knees as he planned to get into the stream to rinse off the oppressive feeling that was weighing down his chest. As he dipped his hands into the water, he heard someone call out his name. The ripple of sound seemed to come from under the bridge. Beyond the branches of the willows and ferns growing out of the muddy end of the cemented ledge, he saw Najib, looking taut and drawn, his cheeks scruffy and sunken. 'Come here, Mohsin,' he whispered urgently. 'NOW!'

There was a fire in his eyes. Without unfolding his rolled-up trousers, Mohsin stepped into the water and waded downstream.

As he moved under the bridge, he saw the two boys, Nazir and Imtiyaz, also there wearing hangdog expressions. They were standing on the ledge, and around their feet were wet heaps of rocks they had collected from the bed of the stream.

'What's this all about?' Mohsin frowned at Najib.

'Don't you know?'

'What's this about?' Mohsin repeated, raising his voice. Over the bridge, a huge truck rumbled past.

'That sick, son-of-a-bitch. We're planning to teach him a lesson.'

'I'm going to throw the first rock,' Nazir said, thumping his chest.

'I'll throw the second one,' Imtiyaz said.

'And as his car slows down,' Najib said, 'you'll have to drop a huge, huge rock from the roof of my shop on to the roof of his car.'

Mohsin felt the blood rushing through him. The naked rage in the eyes of the two boys fascinated him. Mohsin picked up a stone and regarded it for a moment before nodding to Najib. Najib lit a cigarette. He drew a long puff and as he blew the smoke out, he spat into the water. 'Sick son-of-a-bitch,' he muttered.

At that moment, Mohiddin began his mournful call for prayer in the mosque. His voice, reverberating over the city, struck Mohsin below the bridge. Making an instant decision, Mohsin shook the hands of the two boys and Najib and hastily walked out of there.

He mounted the bank, performed his ablutions quickly and returned to the road. He ran into the market and was almost hit by a white jeep.

'D'you want to fuckin' die?' Force 10 shouted. Mohsin threw a glance at him but did not stop. He crossed the road and entered the mosque.

He walked to the front and sat down beside Mohiddin, who smiled at him. Mohsin sat in silence composing himself. Then, as Mohiddin started reciting, *'Ya Rasullallah, Ya Rasullallah,'* he clutched his hand and recited the incantation along with him.

9
The Cowherd

❧

At sixty, he was still the cowherd of Kanelwan. His real name was Mohammad Sultan Sheikh but everyone in the village called him Sul Watul. He was wiry, with enormous eyes and a hunchback. His sharp chin jutted out below his sunken cheekbones. He wore a grimy conical cap to cover his bald head. Years of consuming snuff had blackened his teeth and given him an ulcerous mouth. The corners of his lips trembled as he spoke, the words emerging in rancid, frothy torrents.

That morning he sat hunched in the cold, dark kitchen. As the corners of his lips began to tremble, Gulam, his son, glanced sideways at Halim in the corner. She nudged the ladle-like skewer, *krootcsh,* into the mouth of the mud oven and twisted the long handle. The twigs crackled and a flame leapt above the cauldron of tea. She dished bright embers of charcoal into the firepot.

'Gulam, give this to Baba,' she said to her husband.

Sultan snatched the *kangid* from Gulam and instead of putting it inside his pheran, he raised it over his head saying, 'I want to burn Anzar Shah's beard. He stole my grandson from me and shut down my business. Who do I play with? What will we eat?'

There was a long silence. Then Sultan said, 'His mother's roasted cunt.'

Halim covered her mouth with her scarf in shame, fixing her eyes on the smouldering fire. Gulam rose and held his father. He pressed down Sultan's arm that was shaking with rage and lowered the fire-pot to the floor.

Sultan hissed in air through the gaps in his clenched teeth. He glared at his son and grabbed him by the scruff of his neck.

'I told you not to touch me, you coward,' he shouted.

Halim hurriedly positioned herself between the two men. 'We'll find something, Baba,' she cried, trying to prise Sultan's hard hands from around her husband's throat. 'If nothing works, I'll go begging in the village.'

Gulam's face swelled, his eyes bulging.

'Baba, Baba, for God's sake,' Halim pleaded, 'let him go.'

'I want my grandson back,' Sultan shouted, pushing his son away. 'Why don't you go and bring Jamshid back from that vile preacher.'

Gulam ran out of the kitchen and stood gasping for breath on the flat rock outside the entrance door. He straightened his hurting neck, breathing hard.

Halim came out and gave him a glass of water.

'He is becoming a beast,' Gulam said, swallowing the water, his voice hoarse.

'If we don't bring Jamshid back, that is fine. But we do have to do something about the food,' Halim said.

'Let him starve. Fucking, filthy *watul.*'

'He's your father.' Halim took the glass from him and went back inside.

Gulam's feet were freezing. He went into the corridor where he had put his rubber shoes and slipped them on. He sank into the snow up to his shins as he walked out into the vast grove surrounding the house. It was a forest of mute trees, with trunks grey and bone-coloured, and bare branches laden with snow. He leaned against the trunk of an old elm. He was breathing calmly now. The air was crisp and he could see far. When he looked back at his house, it stood out like a dirty-grey hayrick in a pristine, white jungle. To the rear were elms leading to the pasture around which wound the Jhelum, dry and diminished at this time of the year. Three days ago, when it had not snowed and the ground was dry, it was there to the riverbank almost two miles to the north, that Sultan had dragged the cow soon after it had died. It was there that he had repeatedly suggested they go after the food in the house had been depleted.

Gulam knew the cow. It had belonged to Rafiq Galwan. It was a lithe, black animal with a big white spot on its forehead. Over the last several years, it had calved thirteen times, yielding hundreds of kilos of milk to the family. Rafiq Galwan could have sold it to the butcher as it grew old, but he showed exceptional mercy and allowed the cow to age, feeding it fresh bales of grass, even after its udder had dried up completely. He asked Sultan to take it away from the byre as soon as it died. 'Do not skin her,' he had told him. 'Just take her away from here.'

Gulam shuddered as he imagined the carcass, its eyes sad and shiny. I'm not going to go anywhere near there, no matter what, he thought.

He turned around and looked westward. The gulf between his house and the village seemed even wider because of the difficulty of trudging through the snow. The spire of the mosque steepled to the sky beside Rafiq Galwan's three-storeyed, concrete house. The house had a winged roof of corrugated tin sheets almost as high as the spire. Rafiq had the biggest paddy farm in the village of two hundred households. He owned four cows and dozens of sheep and goats. He was prosperous because he was the most devout *murid* of Syed Anzar Shah.

Last summer, one bright June afternoon, Gulam walked Jamshid to the village. As the two emerged from the grove, they saw Syed Anzar Shah. He was a tall, wide-shouldered man and walked with a light step. His bright face was covered with a white broom of beard. He was clad in a starched white shalwar kameez and black shoes of soft leather, and a black vest. A high, blond karakul crowned his head.

Gulam was awestruck. He slowed down, gripping his son's wrist. It was said that Syed Anzar Shah had the power to communicate with jinns. Whenever a jinn transgressed and entered the domain of humans, he was the man to be consulted. He tamed the evil jinns; he fought with them by chanting the knots of words from his rosary. In the little town of Bijbyor across the river, people thronged to his house, Syed Manzil. Young girls in love babbling gibberish at night; men struck with losses in business; housewives with difficult calves; infertile couples; and the heads of the households whose families were held in thrall under dark spells of sorcery.

Gulam led his son to the entrance door of the mosque only after Anzar Shah had disappeared inside.

'I'll return after an hour and meet you here,' he said, kissing the boy's head. 'Don't play with the village kids. Do you remember the last time when Suhail Galwan called you *watul*?' Suhail Galwan, who had hurled the casteist slur on Jamshid, was Rafiq Galwan's grandson.

'I won't, Father,' Jamshid promised and went inside. Suhail Galwan was sitting in the first row near where Anzar Shah was seated on a high wooden chair. Jamshid kept his distance and subsided to the last row.

As Anzar Shah began to recite from the Qur'an, he noticed Jamshid. The kid was aloof and sitting apart.

Anzar Shah stopped chanting and asked Jamshid to stand up. He asked him his name and the name of his father.

If Syed was at the top of the echelon among the castes in Kashmir, Sheikh lurked somewhere near the bottom. If *pir* signified knowledge, purity and culture, *watul* denoted the stink of faeces, scavenging and raw leather.

While the other boys and girls in class could not stop whispering, Jamshid sat quietly awaiting his turn in his place. And when it came, he stood up, clasped his hands over his navel, closed his eyes and recited 'The Cow', accurately reproducing the 286 verses of the longest chapter from his prodigious memory. The boy's sweet voice dazzled Anzar.

The next day, soon after the Friday prayers, Rafiq Galwan entered the kitchen. The strong fellow seemed shattered.

'Sultan ... congratulations,' he said.

'What for?' Gulam asked.

'Today, while delivering the sermon in the mosque in Bijbyor, Syed Anzar said that he has chosen Jamshid as his disciple. He wants him to live with their family in Syed Manzil where he'll teach him the Qur'an.'

'He must be joking,' Sultan said.

'Really?' Gulam asked Rafiq. 'You shut up, Baba.'

'Yes. He sent me to fetch the lad,' Rafiq Galwan said.

'Is Anzar Shah still encouraging you to buy hides from us watals, Rafiq?' Sultan interrupted.

'He had nothing to do with that and that is not why I have stopped buying from you.'

'Can you tell me why?' Sultan persevered.

Rafiq did not explain. He rose to leave.

'Please stay and have tea with us,' Halim said.

'Some other time, I need to go now,' Rafiq replied.

'Let him go back to his *pir*,' Sultan said. Then to Gulam and Halim, 'He won't tell you, but I will. Anzar Shah is building a shop by the highway. While the father sells verses of the Qur'an he has written on small paper chits, *taweez*, his son will sell the shoes made in the factories of Punjab. Anzar Shah broke his deal with the shoemakers of Srinagar to whom he sold the hides that he bought from Rafiq.'

The couple ignored Sultan's bellyaching and went into their room. They sat on the mattress on the floor, with Jamshid between them, a primer in his hand.

'The old man keeps babbling,' Gulam said. 'Don't ever listen to what he says.'

'Our Jamshid is very fortunate,' Halim said, smiling and stroking her son's head.

The next morning, all spruced up, they took him to Rafiq Galwan's house. He was standing in the courtyard, examining the cracks in the wall of the cowshed.

'Don't heed my father,' Gulam said to him by way of greeting.

'Useless and bitter,' Rafiq replied. 'But don't worry. I'll take your son to my pir right now.'

The couple thanked him and, kissing Jamshid many times, they walked back home. Their hearts were filled with a sad, overflowing joy. How was it possible that an all-important man like Syed Anzar Shah should pay their son any attention? How did this miracle happen?

As soon as they reached home, Gulam, who had never spoken to Anzar Shah, began to think of thanking him in person. He needed to find him a gift.

'You should ask Rafiq for work,' Halim suggested.

So back he went, to ask for work. Rafiq was stingy and reluctant. Gulam had to negotiate hard until Rafiq agreed to give him the task of repairing the wall.

At the end of his two-week stint, cutting hay and preparing clay to stack the fresh bricks, instead of money, Gulam asked Rafiq for a lamb.

'I'll give you a lamb, but you owe me one complete month of labour,' Rafiq replied.

Gulam agreed and took the white-fleeced lamb home where Halim fed it green willow leaves and lined its eyes with kohl and daubed its hooves with henna. The very next day, a Friday, Gulam put on his best kameez and shalwar and set off for Bijbyor with the lamb in his lap.

A passenger boat ferried him across the river. He entered a wide street lined with shops on either side. He recognized Anzar Shah's voice booming out of the loudspeaker. He made his way along the edge of the highway, a group of six children followed him, heckling and bleating like roused lambs. They trailed him up to the mosque.

Gulam cursed them as he opened the picketed gate and quickly walked in. He strode across the lawns and mounted the stairs leading to the veranda. When he turned around, to his relief the gang of children had disappeared. Little bastards of Bijbyor, he thought. Town boys making fun of a village bumpkin.

He put the lamb down on the steps, holding on to its ear, in order to remove his shoes. Through the loudspeaker, Anzar Shah continued his sermon:

'Those who make a living by skinning dead animals, those who make leather by plunging into stinking ditches, are committing an act that is impure, *makruh*. It is as disgusting to me as adultery. In my area, in all our thirty-four villages surrounding our little pure town of Bijbyor, these people must abstain from this contaminating practice. They must or we will see what to do with them.'

Gulam was startled. He pictured his father's face, furrowed in rage. The lamb shook its head, making Gulam lose his grip on its ear. He chased after it with one shoe as it gambolled away on to the highway where a speeding truck ran over it.

ॐ

When Gulam returned home, he went directly to his room. Halim was lying on the mattress on the floor. Her face was pale and her eyes were sunken. As the winter deepened and their stock of food dwindled, her hips narrowed and her skin became dry and desiccated.

'I am going to faint with hunger,' she said, grabbing Gulam's arm. 'I wonder why Syed Anzar Shah prohibits eating a dead animal when we have to kill it anyway?'

'The old man has corrupted you,' Gulam said to his wife and left the room.

When he entered the kitchen, his father taunted him. 'Even the strongest men become meek in their women's beds.'

'Fine.' Gulam sighed, giving in. He too was feeling frustrated with hunger.

The snowflakes were drifting down from a sky luminescent with a soft, white light. Gulam followed his father to the pasture. On the way, he glanced back once and saw in the distance the roof of Rafiq Galwan's house. Smoke was rising from the chimney, pushing the snowflakes upwards. He wondered what kind of sumptuous dinner was being cooked there. His mouth watered and his stomach rumbled. A snow-laden bough broke with a loud crack and a dog howled in the distance.

It took them almost an hour to reach the riverbank where the cow's carcass lay, covered with a shroud of fresh snow. Had it been summer, the shrivelled old beast would have gone sour and putrid in the heat because of the open wounds caused by the jagged rocks on the ground as Sultan dragged it. It would have attracted and maddened the village dogs feasting on its flesh.

Sultan wiped the tip of his nose, pink and runny in the cold, with the coarse sleeve of his pheran. He dusted off the snow from the corpse's neck and handed Gulam the axe.

Gulam struck a blow but nothing happened.

'You're hopeless,' Sultan said, snatching the axe from him. He flung his pheran on the snow. Then, taking a deep, contemplative breath, he delivered terribly strong blows on the carcass. An entire flank came loose.

Gulam picked it up and, stepping away from his father, put it on his shoulder.

Sultan raised the axe higher, delivering blow after blow upon the dead beast, hitting its head and haunches. He struck it along the spine repeatedly. He turned red in the face and his breath became hoarse. But he did not stop; he continued to hack away at the animal's belly, spilling out its entrails.

It was getting dark and the snow had stopped falling.

'Come, let us go now, Baba,' Gulam said. 'We have enough meat. Let us go home, Baba.'

Sultan was deaf to his son's calls. His eyes filled with tears and he threw the axe away. He picked up the pieces of meat he had shredded and hurled them at the trees. With his bare hands, he dug out the guts from the cow's belly and flung them on to the branches of the surrounding trees. He scampered about, yammering to the trees, laughing and crying simultaneously as night fell.

10
The Nightmares of Major S

~❧~

At three o'clock in the morning, Major S was startled awake with the sound of a crash. As he returned to consciousness, he took control in the pitch-dark of the room; he did not bother to even pull out the torch from the top drawer of the cabinet. In a combat zone, where everything was in surreptitious motion, a slim shaft of light could be shattered by a barrage of bullets. He grabbed his gun from under his pillow and threw himself off the bed. He crawled towards the rear wall and positioned himself between the heater and the window. He was ready to shoot now. He waited for the slightest stirring, waited for it to come at him again, but the sound had vanished into the dead of the night.

Major S touched the cylindrical heater with the tip of his gun. It made a hollow sound; at the bottom, the embers of coal had turned into a mound of ash. His legs and feet were cold and he realized that he was clad only in underpants. He rolled back on the wooden floor, his forefinger curled around the trigger. Although he wanted to immediately summon Arvind who was dozing in the corridor, he decided to put on some clothes first.

As he sat on the bed, it came again. This time the impact was so great that the entire roof shuddered. A bull, it seemed, had butted its horned head onto the thin corrugated tin. Angry and charged, he heard the roar of the waking soldiers in the other rooms of the mansion and in the tents in the courtyard. He stood up, kicked the window open and knelt by the windowsill. He fired in the direction of the river and the willows beyond the water. He raised his gun and fired it into the vast silent sky trailed with snowflakes. As soon as he had used up all his bullets, he dipped to the floor, lest the rebels, following the sparks, should rip his head open. Just then, the door behind him opened. He spun around so quickly, he could have thrown his gun with force and precision at the forehead of the person entering had he not cried: 'It's me, Arvind, sir.' And to clear Major S's confusion, added with haste, 'The rebellious weather of this place! The snow is so heavy that it's breaking the branches of the sycamore.'

Major S sighed in relief. Then realizing it *was* Arvind, he said, 'Get out of here!'

When the day broke, it stopped snowing. Major S burst into the adjacent bedroom. 'Cut the fucking tree down, Sunil,' he said to the subedar, walked out onto the veranda and sat cross-legged on a chair with his customary scowl. Past the torments of the nightmare, which seemed distant after a spell of deep sleep, he became grimly serene. He called to Arvind to pour him a cup of tea from the kettle that he had placed on the table.

Sunil emerged from the house and saluted Major S. He was tall and hefty, and prompt to jump blindly to his officer's bidding. He walked into the tent besides the courtyard and reappeared with an axe. Under the gigantic, grey-trunked tree with it monstrously large white branches, Sunil looked like an ant. Major S nodded at him and raised his cup. 'Cut the bastard down!' he commanded.

Sunil attacked the trunk, striking forcefully, sending the pieces of white and reddish pulp flying about the courtyard.

ॐ

As the winter deepened, Major S consolidated his camp, imposing an order of harsh solidity. To fortify the walls of the discoloured and dilapidated colonial mansion, the rotting wooden planks were sawed off and the gaps were filled with shingle and cement. The rugs and round pillows filled with hardened rat shit were replaced with iron beds with spring mattresses and thick bed sheets patterned with swirling, olive-green leaves. On the kitchen shelves the dusty shards of English crockery, the remains of cups, demitasses and blue porcelain vases, were replaced with steel mugs. The place received a thorough spring cleaning destroying cobwebs and the nests of bats and swallows hanging from the ceiling. The doors and windows were rehinged; they swung swiftly to the beat of the new militarized time.

The courtyard and the surrounding lawns were overgrown with willows that had not been cut down since the time of the exodus of the Mughals from Kashmir. The generations of sparrows nesting in them carried the burden and guilt of witnessing the concubines – Muslim, Hindu, Zoroastrian, Christian – getting raped, their shrieks during the assaults rising and lingering above the leaves. Beneath, the slothful kings and pot-headed princes reclined on their elbows, relishing the reek of cum. In the beginning, even Major S was astonished at where he was, at the concubine's screams that entered and further disrupted the discordant logic of his recurring nightmares. So, he summoned the imam of the mosque that the mansion faced across the highway. Syed Anzar Shah was the only man in town who was conscious of the magnitude of his power and expected the major to address him with the conviviality of a friend. However, he was denied even the acknowledgement of eye contact. Major S told him in a cold voice to summon all Bijbyor's young men before showing the imam to the door. Syed Anzar Shah nevertheless made the announcement from his pulpit, his voice bruised and booming through the loudspeaker fitted to the spire of the mosque. Within minutes, young men queued outside what would become the camp. The photographs and names on the identity cards were matched with their real faces and the names they uttered were matched with the letters that formed their names on their identity cards. If the interrogating soldier thought there was a mismatch, the men were slapped, kicked, harassed and held accountable for a crime that more than an act of conscious deception evoked the classical breach between the signifier and the signified which the French semioticians after Saussure would be fondly attracted to explore. The ones that passed the test were registered with precision, under the gaze of the soldier, on a long ledger with an impenetrable green cover. Each individual's existence, reduced to a name and number, was caged in complex tables. Along with the men of military, the young men were then directed to cut down the willow – the very same willows under whose twilit canopy they had met their sweethearts and their hearts, secretly rebelling against the social codes of religion, had palpitated with the possibilities of stealing inside the mansion into the blissful dark for a kiss – and dig pits where the iron pillars were to be erected into the ground. Sitting in a chair on the veranda, smoking his cigarette, Major S oversaw the snow and earth being flung about by the shovels as the rain-proof sheets of tarpaulin were hung over the pillars. A gun tower was erected where the sycamore had stood. Four bunkers were set up at each of the four corners of the camp. Empty flour bags were stuffed with sand of bullet-stopping density and the bunkers were joined with high walls of the most obdurate concrete, their tops whorled with barbed wire that looped high in the air, entangling the skies.

On a March afternoon, it finally stopped snowing and started raining. Arvind brought out tea to the veranda. He was twenty-two years old; a quiet, lean, dark, diminutive fellow with sad eyes and a feeble voice. He had joined the army a year before as a lance-naik but Major S had turned him into his sponge boy. His duty was to listen to Major S's rants and absorb the dark syrup of anger that coursed through Major S's veins. Arvind remained in the corridor, rooted to the major's wooden shoe rack that held the innumerable pairs of lumberjack boots and leather shoes, the cleaning rag flung over his scrawny shoulder. Upon their arrival in Kashmir, something significant had happened. Something had changed and Major S had altered his role. He asked Arvind to cook for him, without finding it odd that the food he ate was touched, cleaned and kneaded by an outcaste.

As soon as Major S finished his tea, he rose and tossed the stub of the burning cigarette into the slush. He grabbed Arvind's wrist and said, with the earnestness of a pundit, 'I want to show you something.' He led him straight to his bedroom window and flung it open. He pointed to the Jhelum, swollen and flooded.

'What do you see, Arvind?' he asked.

'Sir, a lot of muddy water,' Arvind said.

'You dumbass!' Major S bellowed.

'Sir, sir …' Arvind stuttered.

'Centuries ago this was all clear water, and not a bit of it was muddy. This entire fucking valley was serene water touched by the crystalline soles of Parvati floating over the lake. After salvaging it, a pious rishi asked the brahmins to settle here. But now, the water is gone. And what remains?'

Arvind looked at him, unsure and terrified.

'This fucking river remains. And everywhere, there is creepy vegetation. When the rains stop and the sun comes out, you will see the green invade the banks and those hills in the distance. Thousands of shrubs, creepers and disgusting grasses and nettles will sprout.'

Arvind nodded, although he had never heard the story of Parvati. It was not his family's folklore.

'You don't understand, you are an idiot,' Major S snarled. 'Get out of here!'

'Yes, sir,' Arvind said, bowing and leaving the room.

It continued to rain throughout the day. In the evening, as Major S walked into the courtyard, Arvind held an umbrella over him. He went around the camp once, checking on the soldiers, peering into the sheds on either side and the bunkers. He returned to the mansion and asked Arvind to give him dinner. After dinner, he retired to bed early.

He dreamt of a sunny March morning. Bathed, shaved and clad in a clean uniform, he was seated on the veranda. The sunlight poured out on the courtyard. A smiling and placid Arvind emerged from the house.

'Good morning, sir,' he said and placed the tea tray with cup, kettle and biscuits on the table.

As Major S raised the cup to his lips, a flurry of shining grass blades sprouted in the ground before his amazed eyes. He glanced at Arvind and noticed that he didn't seem alarmed.

'Can't you fucking see the mutiny in the making? The rishi had a reason for inviting only brahmins and not chamars to occupy the drying satisar.'

Arvind vanished and Major S was thrown off the veranda. Beneath a dark, overcast sky, he was dragged naked and cold along the ground covered with sharp blades of grass.

He woke up to the sound of his own terrified howls. He was covered in sweat and his heart and hands were shaking with a dark sense of foreboding. He came out into the corridor and kicked Arvind awake.

'Get me a shovel, right now,' he shouted.

Arvind woke up and knuckled the sleep from his eyelids.

'Get me a shovel,' Major S repeated.

Arvind sprang to his feet and ran out to the shed and returned with a shovel. Major S walked bare-footed into the courtyard. It was still raining. He struck the wet earth and overturned the soil. The soldiers slowly came out of their sheds and bunkers, lighting their torches, and watched in bewildered silence. Sunil brought another shovel and joined Major S. They dug up the entire courtyard. In the morning, Major S telephoned a man in the high command in New Delhi.

'I want a truck of red sandstone now. This is urgent.'

As soon as he fell asleep that night, the nightmare returned. He was thrown into a terrain of darkness, bristling with sabre-sharp blades of grass by an invisible hand that dragged him through a meadow, over a white wooden fence, and towards the spectre of a Mughal dismounting from a young, wailing concubine. The sparrows flew out of the absent willows in sharp gusts, cheeping in lament. Major S tore himself out of his sleep and telephoned the high command again.

'Fuckers! Send it now or we lose the courtyard!'

The truck arrived after two days and halted at the gate of the camp. Although it was still raining torrentially, Major S went out to welcome the driver in person. He told Arvind to make tea for him and give him sweets.

In a matter of minutes, Major S rallied his soldiers who stood scattered around in the courtyard like a group of lost children, the rain dripping on their sagging heads and trickling down their wary faces, their hearts sullen, dull and confounded by the confinement of the camp.

'I want every inch of the courtyard to be covered,' Major S addressed them from the height of the veranda. 'I don't want even a single gap to allow even a single blade of grass to grow.'

The courtyard was covered with sandstone inch by inch. Major S went into his room and took out a bottle of whiskey from the closet. He drank deeply. Then, taking a deep breath, he lay on his bed without removing his shoes. He thought of calling Arvind to untie his laces and take his shoes off, but then he let it go. He was feeling warm in his feet and light in his head. He stared fixedly at the small, tricolour that he had spread on the wall in front of the bed. He drank on and the flag expanded to extend from one end of the wall to the other, from the top to the bottom; the black circle in the middle enlarged and its spokes began to move. He recollected the rigorous training session at the Military Academy in Dehradun that he had attended two years ago at the end of which the flag had been awarded to him. He still remembered the words his officer had said: 'Either we uphold this flag or come back shrouded in it.' After a night of heavy drinking and his failure to spend the night with a young, slim girl with wide hips because a mole visible on her waist when he had undressed her looked disturbingly familiar, he had flown to New Delhi on the earliest flight the next morning, the flag tidily folded in the briefcase tucked under his arm. He had dozed during the flight and was woken an hour later, disoriented and groggy, by the announcement of the landing. He looked out through the window at the clump of green trees and cluster of brown box-like, flat-roofed houses caught in a cloud of hot, thick smoke. He had come to the city during his youth from a village in Bihar, fleeing an old, ailing, poor, landless father, who, at the end of his career as a meagre politician, had given himself to Nehruvian Fabianism. His father had irritated Major S beyond belief. During the initial days when he was adrift and restless in the city, Major S had met Radhika whom he knew he was going to marry the instant their eyes met.

As he walked out of the airport and sat back in the black and yellow taxi, he thought about his empty apartment in Vasant Vihar. He felt strange and weak and was engulfed by an unexpected deluge of emotions. He pulled himself together, stretching his broad shoulders, his officer's words resounding in his head. He clenched his hands to hold back the weak tears.

In about twenty minutes he reached the apartment and, as he stepped out of the taxi, a fresh shiver of memory ran through him. He shook his head hard, slapping his cheek as he handed the fare to the cabbie who thought Major S had been bitten by a mosquito. He clutched the handle of his briefcase and ascended the staircase to the third floor of the quiet, grey-distempered building.

Over the entrance door, the wall sported a wet stain around a deep fissure. He grunted at the cracks that branched off from the fissure in the middle into the paint dampened by the water. He entered the living room where he was overpowered by the smell of dust and disuse. He sneezed as he walked into the bedroom. He put his briefcase on the bed before returning to the living room to switch on the lights and the ceiling fan.

A huge cockroach awaited him in the kitchen sink. It lay on its back, its legs twitching. He squashed its head with a steel ladle and discarded the carcass in the trash-bin.

As he switched on the fridge, he saw a picture pasted to the door. Megha, just three at the time, was on his lap, and Radhika stood leaning towards him. All three of them were smiling, their eyes reflecting the flashlight. He tore the picture from the fridge and threw it into the trash-bin.

In the evening, when the house grew cooler and the smell of the dust had subsided, he poured himself a glass of brandy. He sat on the sofa and turned on the TV. They were showing *Rope* on Star Movies, the movie he had watched with Radhika, Megha and Megha's boyfriend, Vijay, who had come to visit the previous year. Afterwards, when Radhika had told him about Megha's wish to marry Vijay, a silence had overcome him. When she repeated the question, he stared at her blankly like a child unable to comprehend the question. And then he told her in a voice that would brook no arguments that the boy needed to be an army man which Vijay clearly was not. Intense arguments had ensued until he hit Radhika in a rage. She was shocked into silence.

'I always believed that you'd never do that to me,' she had whispered. 'You have changed so much.' She divorced him and went away with Megha to live at the faculty lounges of Delhi University. Major S's father was dead but his mother was alive. He had rented a house for her in Patna and arranged for a servant to help around the house. He visited her regularly and paid her expenses with the same passion with which every time Major S had leaned towards his father in his childhood, she had flogged his palms and buttocks with a switch. She had been furious in evoking loyalty; she had punished her son because she felt her husband, with his empty rhetoric and socialist ideals, had betrayed and belied her expectations. Despite her senescence with cataracts in both the eyes that had witnessed her husband's deterioration as he wilted away, she still held herself with the hauteur of an entitled brahmin, in the way she sat Zohra Sehgal style in a chair, draped in a white sari, her gold-bangled arms neatly folded in her lap. Just before he had left for Dehradun for the two-month-long training she had called him and told him that Megha had come to visit her before leaving to study in New York.

During the commercial break, Major S fetched the whiskey bottle and a glass with ice cubes. He remembered Brandon. Not just for his blue suit and sharp tie, but Brandon's ability to be calm and grinning while helping Phillip to place David in the chest. Major S was not very sure where the movie was set. He did not know that Megha lived in the same neighbourhood in Manhattan where the movie took place. Had he called her, he might have confessed that missing her frightened him. From her descriptions of the place, he might have wondered that she was lodging in one of the buildings visible from the wide window, from where the smoke spiralled out of the chimneys, as Brandon pulled the curtains open to dispel the dark and soothe Philip's discomposure. But, as Brandon put the candle stands on the chest, Major S did wonder about the length of the chest. Six feet or less, he reckoned, since David's legs had to be bent to fit inside.

During the movie, Major S fell asleep. He was awoken when the bell buzzed and Rupert returned to the apartment. Major S watched the end bleary-eyed: Rupert emptying his gun, the police cars wailing and their lights flashing in the background.

Major S saw the casket again in his dream that night. It was in the middle of his living room. Radhika was sitting on the sofa across from him, reading her students' papers. She was lost in her own work and did not pay attention to what lay in front of her. But Major S did. He saw the chest. It was right there. How could she ignore it? He moved towards it and Radhika covered her face with her sari. Major S raised the lid.

He saw Vijay's naked back and Megha, equally naked, emerged from beneath him. He saw the mole on her waist. Their arms and legs entwined, as Megha moaned ecstatically, pouting her moist lips.

Amazed, Major S looked up at Radhika, but she had vanished. Only her sob rose from the crumpled mound of her sari and the white litter of papers. With the dark syrup of rage pumping through his veins, his eyes bulged and his body trembled. He ran into the bedroom and grabbed his gun suspended from the ceiling by a white rope. He returned to the living room, but the chest had disappeared. He could not find it; where the hell did Brandon and Philip hide it? He ran from one room to the other, running headlong into Rupert.

'Who the fuck are you?' Rupert asked, kissing Mrs Atwater, whom he held in his arms. 'No, no more Nietzsche. No more lessons in the art of the perfect murder.'

Major S brushed past him and dashed into the bedroom. The chest was there, standing upright, facing away from him, gazing out through the window, like an erect walking coffin. It kept pacing back and forth agitatedly, its lid working loose.

Major S was too terrified to peek inside: to see dead David or Megha and her fucking boyfriend. He stepped closer and fired at it, drilling six holes along its length, in one straight, vertical line.

11
Robin Polish

❧

It dawned blue and gloomy. The shutters of the shops were rolled down and coated with a hoary dust. The only sound besides the sporadic birdsong was the whimpering from across the road. Gulam was familiar with the famished, brown dog. It squatted on the steps of Shirmal Bakery, its tongue lolling between its teeth. 'Who gives a damn about you?' Gulam grunted, sitting down on a torn gunny bag that was his seat and unlatched his worktable. He pulled out the pair of loafers that Jamshid had given him yesterday. He slipped his hand inside one of the shoes and raised it up like a miniature plane. Smelling and feeling the soft leather, he forgot about the dog's whimpers.

Shirmal Bakery was on the ground floor of the two-storeyed building of red, baked bricks cemented together with mud. It had a steep roof of bright, thin, corrugated tin.

A picket door barred the dog from entering the stairwell. When someone clomped down the stairs heavily and pushed open the door, the dog took fright, sprang to its feet and tottered away before returning again to its usual spot.

Nadim crossed the road and greeted Gulam, leaning forward to shake his hand. What brings Misreh's boy here so early? Gulam wondered, studying his face. Nadim, a tall, hot-blooded youth, with an aura of fake genteelness, was a fake rebel. He wore blue, baggy jeans and white sneakers. He had upturned the wide collar of his buttoned shirt. He was not Pakistan-trained; he was not among those who braved the hunger, cold and exhaustion of a trek across the mountains and dared to venture near the death that awaited in the wooded slopes where beasts prowled in the silence of the jungle. The boys were led by the secret guide who carried a small sack of almonds and candies and kept a rope with him. The guide made sure to feed the boys but he also strangled the ones who got too tired and could not keep up with the rest of the group. He hung them from the branch of a tree to prevent any chance of them relaying information to the soldiers about the secret route taken across the Line of Control. Nadim too had disappeared for a while but rumour had it that he had trained in the sweet shade of the pasture across the Jhelum, carrying guns and water bottles for Showkat, the real commander. However, the instant Nadim was back in Bijbyor, he proclaimed himself a full-fledged rebel. To refute this, gangs of snickering children trailed after him, calling him, *Pasture, Pasture, Pasture*. 'Bastards,' he cursed, spitting and shooing them away by pretending to hurl a stone at them.

'What have you boys been up to?' Gulam asked Nadim.

'We're busy organizing the meetings of the Jammu Kashmir Students' Front,' he replied.

'That I can see. Jamshid hardly has any time for me these days,' Gulam complained.

'For all your sarcasm one day you'll see how wrong you were. One day when we bring independence to Kashmir and Jamshid becomes our first prime minister. He is marked for greatness and is destined to make history.'

'It's too early to say that.'

'Aazadi is around the corner.'

'I don't know about that. I don't see it anywhere near me.'

Nadim paused, lowering his voice. 'You should meet Anzar Shah.'

'For what?'

'To talk about Jamshid's marriage.'

If Jamshid marries, Gulam thought with a thrill of anticipation, he'll leave Shah Manzil, build a separate house and ask me to live with him.

'Do I need to talk to Anzar Shah about the nikah?' Gulam asked.

'Yes, and about Rosy.'

'What did you say?' Gulam asked, puzzled. 'What about Rosy?'

'Jamshid wants to marry her,' Nadim replied.

Gulam looked at him incredulously. 'How dare you even say a thing like that,' Gulam said.

'That is what Jamshid wants,' Nadim said.

'Go away,' snapped Gulam.

'I will, but I thought you should know.' Nadim shrugged. 'Oh, get lost!'

ॐ

At the end of the day, after polishing and patching several pairs of shoes, Gulam tucked an old copy of the daily newspaper *Chattan* under his arm and trudged upstairs to his room, exhausted. He removed his shoes outside the door. Cramped and dark, with a low ceiling of dusty wooden beams, the walls grey and sooty, the room had two peepholes for windows, one in front and the other at the back. He dragged his feet along the rough hay-mat covering the floor and, without pushing the front window open, sat in the corner. He put the newspaper down and sighed as he propped his head on his hands, sinking his elbows into a grimy pillow. He felt forlorn and numb. A dull sleep was about to overcome him when the door opened.

'Assalamu aliakum,' Jamshid greeted his father.

'Wa-aliakum,' Gulam mumbled.

'I've brought something for you, Father,' Jamshid said, smiling broadly, holding up a haunch of beef wrapped in an old newspaper.

Gulam watched him curiously, feeling his weight gathering and concentrating on his thin forearm. Jamshid was a broad-shouldered young man now, twice the size of his father. He was six feet tall and had long, strong limbs. He was clad in neatly ironed white kameez and shalwar. The Syeds had fed and schooled him well. His hair, thick and curly like his father's, was groomed and he gave off a strong whiff of perfume.

'The shoes are ready,' Gulam said coldly.

'I'll collect them tomorrow. But today, right now, I am going to cook for you, Father. And I am going to stay the night,' Jamshid announced.

Did the Syeds kick you out when they came to know that you want to marry Rosy? Gulam wondered.

'I'm tired,' he said aloud, 'do whatever you like.'

Jamshid opened the rear window. A kerosene stove was placed beside the two wooden shelves at the far end of the room. There were little glass jars filled with spices on the lower shelf: yellow turmeric, red chili powder, green aniseed, green cardamom and black cardamom. He found a wooden-handled knife behind the jars and rummaged around for an onion in a bag on the upper shelf. As he deftly chopped it up, tears welled up in his smarting eyes. He muffled an involuntary cry. Gulam rose in alarm, but then held back, watching his son in pain.

'It is nothing, Father,' Jamshid said, tearing a scrap of the wet newspaper to wrap it around his bleeding fingertip.

Later, in the dim light of the lantern hitched to a nail in the middle of the ceiling beam, they ate white rice and a dark reddish meat stew.

'Did Nadim come here in the morning, Father?' Jamshid asked.

'Yes, he did,' Gulam replied.

'It is impossible to persuade Syed Anzar Shah and the rest of the family even if you go in person and beg for the hand of their daughter.'

'When it comes to marriage, Sheikhs have no business talking with Syeds,' Gulam replied, glancing away from his son. After a moment of uneasy silence, Gulam rose with his plate and went to the rear window.

'*Koosh, koosh, koosh,*' he called the dog lying somewhere in the dark. It limped into view, wagging its tail in anticipation of food.

Gulam pushed the bones off the edge of his plate and watched them drop to the ground.

'I'm sorry, Father,' Jamshid said as Gulam resumed his seat. 'I'll ask Nadim not to bother you again.'

Gulam nodded and ate the rest of the meal in silence. Afterwards, he took his plate to the big pan that Jamshid had placed beneath the shelves and began to scour it clean. However, his son stopped him.

'I'll wash it, Father,' he said.

Gulam nodded and receded to his corner. He opened his copy of *Chattan* and read while Jamshid did the dishes.

The next morning, by the time he woke up, Jamshid had left. He descended the old creaking staircase and sat at his worktable. As he placed a shoe for re-soling on the desk, a door across the street opened and out walked 'Pasture'. He crossed the road quickly and hurried over.

'Where's Jamshid?' he asked.

'You always frighten the poor dog!' Gulam complained, watching it limp away.

'Fuck the dog! Where the hell is your son?'

He took out a pistol from his pocket and rubbed its barrel with his fingers. For a moment Gulam thought that this was some sick joke. However, when 'Pasture' lit a cigarette, and blew out smoke rings, his tone became menacing. Gulam understood that his loyalties had switched overnight.

'Tell your son to keep away from Rosy,' he said.

If it wasn't for that donkey's dick you hold in your hand, Gulam thought, I'd slap you square in the face. 'I'll tell him whatever you want me to tell him,' he said, nodding at 'Pasture'.

In the evening when Jamshid returned, Gulam grabbed his arm.

'Pasture was here,' he stuttered, his eyes filling with tears.

'Who was here?'

'Pasture … Nadim Pasture.'

'What did he say?'

'He said he'll kill you if you do not keep away from Rosy.'

'I cannot believe he said that,' Jamshid said, hugging Gulam tightly. 'But I'll talk to him, Father.' Gulam almost wrenched himself from his son's embrace.

Jamshid told his father about his being elected the president of Jammu Kashmir Students Front with a roaring, unanimous vote in Rasool Mir College. He had the charm, grace and control of a young man on horseback galloping across a vast field with his countless admirers watching and applauding from the sidelines. Gulam squirmed as every inch of his being rebelled against his son's sangfroid.

The next morning, Jamshid was still asleep when Gulam woke up. He felt a strange reassurance; it had been years since his son had spent two nights in a row at home. He opened the window gently. He had moved to Bijbyor fifteen years ago following his son's arrival in the town.

In the beginning, Jamshid would visit every Sunday but, as he grew older and got more absorbed in the Syed household, his visits became rare. There were times when

he wouldn't visit for months on end. It was during that time
that Gulam began to buy *Chattan* for fifty paise. He vaguely
recalled the Urdu phrases that he had picked up in school
before discontinuing in the fifth grade. He did not feel
important enough to enjoy reading the news. He read to kill
boredom and forget his loneliness.

Thinking back to that time, his stomach roiled with
the memory of the bitter solitude of those nights inside the
room, when darkness mingled with silence and turned into
a viscous, clingy substance that spread all over him, and
permeated his skin into his marrow. He had trembled like a
leaf. He had had an intense desire to speak and be heard. *To
speak and be heard.* He wanted to weep and be heard.

One of those nights, under the mounting weight of his
misery, he felt his chest tighten. As he gasped for breath, a
horrible thought dawned: the light has gone out of my eyes
completely. I have been struck deaf and blind. But before
he could dissolve into nothingness, he jolted himself awake.
Flinging the darned quilt away, he dashed out of the room.
He ran down the staircase and plunged into the street.
He waddled about in the darkness, howling. Then a voice
interrupted him.

'What the hell is wrong with you, Gulamah? Are you
possessed by a jinn?' Misreh asked, touching his shoulder.

Gulam fell silent immediately, becalmed by the softness
of her touch. Her large eyes shimmered bright with the light
of the lantern she held in her hand.

He could not bring himself to speak. She led him by his
arm to the steps of her shop, where the dog was asleep.

'Sit here,' she said quietly, holding his arm.

%

Gulam pushed open the window, letting in the daylight. Where have you been all these years, Jamshid? Why did you ignore me? Were you ashamed that your father is a Sheikh and a *watul*, a dirty, lower-caste cobbler, while you lived with the Syeds?

Despite Gulam's overwhelming shame, he went to Bijbyor because Halim desperately missed Jamshid as only a mother would. She made him buy a gift in the form of a lamb that Gulam lost. What a beautiful lamb it was, a bundle of soft bones wrapped in white fleece. It ran away from Gulam's eager hands towards the highway where a long lumbering truck ran over it, its entrails crushed and blood sticking to the deep grooves of the rubber tyres speeding over the tarmac. Gulam had toiled hard while building the rear wall of Rafiq Galwan's cowshed which had been shattered by the fury of a gale. And sad though Gulam was and empty-handed after the mishap, he went into the mosque's bathrooms where he washed his face and cleansed himself of the dirt that watals were supposed to have deposited not only on their skins but in their souls. He entered the house of God where he dipped his head to the floor and prayed behind Bijbyor's imam who was also his son's saviour, Syed Anzar Shah. However, the prayer did not seem to affect him much. He walked out, an ordinary and unrecognized man, one of a swelling throng of people. He crossed the highway and stood on the bridge as the imam's voice, calm amidst the clamorous songs, continued to praise the Prophet.

The hump-backed bridge was made of wood, entire deodar trees of enormous girth cut down from some distant jungle and planted deep into the ground and river bed. The Jhelum with its sloping banks deepened in the middle. Whether it was the bridge that arched and attained the height or the river that plunged and deepened, Gulam could not tell. As he gripped the railing and gazed at the girders and beams, he was overcome with a dizzy vertigo. The sky was bruisingly bright. The sun, satanic and scorching as it always was on Friday afternoons, speckled the surface of the water. It was probably a reminder from Allah, an indication that Gulam wouldn't be able to save himself from hell, where stones and bones burnt in eternal damnation. The imam was pleading to God. 'For the sake of Muhammad, Allah,' he wept, 'save us, the people of Bijbyor, the people of Kashmir.' His voice had a subtle ferocity now, in addition to the hopeless desperation. It filled Gulam with a nameless dread. The sun shone brighter on the river, devouring the water with its fire.

Gulam heard the lambs bleating in the distance as they were being herded towards the perilous highway where the killer trucks roared past at blazing speed. He teetered at the edge of the bridge, clenching his fists. Although he trembled with fear, he somehow held his ground, a ground that was threatening to crumble beneath his feet.

The imam concluded the prayer and emerged from the mosque to cross the highway surrounded by a cloud of murids, their heads bent in homage as they walked along with him. He walked in the centre and no one dared to walk ahead of him. He was wearing a flowing white robe and light leather chappals. Although many people around him were taller than him, the way he deliberated each step, none were taller in stature.

Gulam retreated to the bridge. He stood erect and with his back pressed to the railing. He bowed to the imam and greeted him loudly. However, his devout entourage had created an impenetrable sound barrier around the holy man. Gulam wanted to raise his voice, but he felt weak and nervous. He watched the imam pass by in a blizzard, white and ethereal.

He climbed to the middle of the bridge. Beneath, he knew, the stones were boiling in the scalding water. The path to the left arced along the shore of the burning river, into a dense profusion of willows.

He tore his eyes away from the water and walked on. Over the multitude of heads bobbing decorously in a divine rhythm, he saw the tall, iron gate painted white. The words 'shah manzil' in Urdu were carved on gleaming, black granite on the pillar to the right.

Gulam entered by the path paved with shingle and lined with flowers. Beds of delicate marigolds and pansies led up to the imposing, concrete house.

Syed Anzar Shah was seated at the far end of the hall on a white lambskin, his back bolstered by a flat pillow. Behind him on the windowsill lay a copy of the Qur'an on its wooden stand. The windows were curtained except the one behind the imam. In the slightly dark room, there was a solemn silence. There seemed to be a consensus among the murids that the silence was only to be broken by the imam's hushed murmurs. The murids, men, women and children, with woeful expressions and dry lips, patiently waited for their turns. The imam, his authority untrammelled and final, checked them one by one, leaning forward to hear their whispers and voice his verdict.

Gulam sat by the door on the carpet. He sidled closer, watching the way the murids thanked the pir by putting money or other offerings, sacks of rice, bags of dry almonds and raw fruit, into his lap. The ones who had come empty handed offered to massage him. He accepted begrudgingly, extending his feet. The murids pressed the pir's sacred shins with their hands and tears of gratitude in their eyes. The pir closed his eyes in ecstasy and mumbled incomprehensible words in Arabic.

Gulam glanced into his eyes. Their immeasurable tranquillity disturbed him.

'Who are you?' the pir asked.

Weak and nervous, Gulam felt at a loss for words. He scratched his ear before stammering that he was Jamshid's father. He wanted to ask the druid how Jamshid was doing, but he could not.

'Your son is gifted,' Syed Anzar Shah said and smiled.

Gulam winced, trying to force a smile. He glanced at the holy man's feet and hesitantly reached for them.

'That is not necessary,' said the pir, asking one of the murids to summon Jamshid.

When he came in with Rosy in tow, the pir said, 'Your father is here,' indicating Gulam, who stood up sweating and indignant ...

In the narrow room, the past hung like a curtain of darkness, the memory an assault – jangling, perpetual and hurtful.

Gulam gulped from Misreh's tumbler that night as she gently caressed the dog's head. He wanted to tell her everything. He wanted to tell her how he missed his wife and son whom he had lost because he was a poor and inadequate man. He wanted to tell her that he found her, Misreh, voluptuous and beautiful, despite his knowledge that she had an affair with Syed Aslam Shah. However, as she sat talking to him in her soft voice, Gulam remained quiet. A slow wind blew through the warm October night, driving the clouds away and the stars reappeared. The wind fluttered the willow branches behind her house, swaying the nests of the sparrows and the bulbuls. A half-moon shone in the sky above the river to the west. Gulam wanted to hold her soft hand and walk with her to the end of the street. He wanted to enter the dense willow coppice where he would pull down her yazar. He wanted to make love to her, tender and furious in turns, murmuring and moaning, for the rest of the night by the bank of the river, as the dew on the dwindling autumn grass moistened their entwined bodies.

Gulam remembered Halim and returned to his room. He shut his eyes and tried to go back to sleep. In the darkness, the floor of the room felt damp. He recalled the winter night. After days of eating scraps of dried bread because nothing was left in the house, Halim was forced to eat a morsel of beef that Gulam's father had torn from a dead cow. She immediately vomited several times, not because the meat was bad, but because she thought she had sinned. She retched as the pungent greenish fluid gushed from her mouth in torrents, staining the bare mud floor.

Gulam held her as she gulped for breath. He lifted her tenderly and put her to bed. He undressed her carefully before covering her emaciated, throbbing and sweating body with blankets.

He hurried to the village, sinking up to his knees in the snow. Half an hour later, he returned freezing but triumphant with some pills and a bottle of milk. He fed her the pills and milk. He kissed her hand and she fell asleep.

However, the next morning, when she opened her eyes, she said, 'I am going back to live with my mother and brothers. I have had enough.'

*

Over the years of living in Bijbyor and polishing Syed Anzar Shah's shoes every time Jamshid brought them along, Gulam's assessment of the imam had changed drastically. Now the imam no longer inspired the dread and awe synonymous with the fear of burning in hellfire. In the rallies and political speeches that Gulam attended, he saw the imam sitting with his friend, Mufti Syed, a shrewd politician who needed no introduction around here, and whose adversaries prayed that his liver would rot with cirrhosis from his secret addiction to whiskey. In the lawns around the mansion, Gulam stole sidelong glances at the imam and realized that despite his powers to exorcise the possessed, he bore an unmistakable resemblance to the flesh-and-blood people surrounding him. Gulam had taught himself to read fluently by regularly reading *Chattan*, and avidly followed the way the imam subtly encouraged the influential and the affluent like Rafiq Galwan's family to vote for Mufti Syed. However, Gulam kept his opinion to himself.

One Friday afternoon, as the imam stood behind the lectern, his hands raised, clearly enunciating the guttural *'ain*'s and *'gain*'s, Gulam stared at him from the last row at the rear corner of the mosque. The huge, rectangular hall was packed with men and was slowly growing more claustrophobic while the imam pontificated about the consequences of disobedience, the wrath of Allah, and the severity of hellfire.

As the sermon continued and the last spot in the mosque was occupied by the last worshipper, the concrete walls, painted smooth and green, began to perspire. The imam's eyes glowed. His brow dampened and his face turned puce. Then all at once, as though slapped by Satan's invisible hand, he fell down in a faint.

The worshippers whispered. Jamshid and Aslam Shah, who were in the first row, raised the prostate preacher to a standing position and dragged him to a chair behind the lectern. Jamshid hurried to the closet in the front wall and brought out a long, glass vial. He uncorked it and sprinkled rosewater on the imam's face.

With fluttering eyes, the imam returned to consciousness. He beckoned to Aslam to draw closer and whispered in his ear. Aslam's eyes hardened, and he shook his head vigorously. He stepped away from his father and whispered into Jamshid's ear.

The murmurs in the great hall died down with Jamshid's first utterance. He took his place behind the lectern and in a calm and assured voice he recited the chapter of 'Joseph' from the Qur'an with such passion that Anzar Shah began to weep.

Gulam, who did not understand Arabic and didn't know what the words meant, felt odd and isolated when all the other worshippers in the mosque began to weep as they recited along with Jamshid. Their supplications irritated him. He knew that 'Pasture', who was also there somewhere in the front row, was sobbing like a child.

As Jamshid's voice rose to a crescendo, the men beat their chests, pleading with Allah for forgiveness. However, Gulam was not moved. He sat cross-legged with his back firmly pressed against the wall. You won't win this time, Jamshid, he thought, not again. He longed to return to his seat of bedraggled gunny bag. He desperately wanted to grab hold of his hammer, spread the hands of both 'Pasture' and Jamshid across the face of his cluttered worktable and smash their knuckles and fingers, releasing little white bones to set sail in pools of blood.

He exited the mosque quietly. Major S watched from the veranda of the bungalow with his binoculars, as Gulam emerged into the lawn and ran down the highway.

The panting and hungry dog at the corner of his street, by the bakery, greeted Gulam, wagging its tail. Gulam knelt with tears in his eyes and hugged the dog. He stroked its back and kissed its cheek. The dog lowered its ears, whining.

'What's the matter, Gulamah?' Misreh asked from behind a basket of shirmals in her bakery. 'Such a show of affection!' Misreh was fresh from a bath and smelt of Hamam soap, her face dusted with white Pond's powder. Big cylindrical earrings dangled from her earlobes.

'Give me a shirmal. Give me two shirmals,' Gulam said urgently, wiping a hanging thread of snot from the dog's mouth.

Misreh emerged through the door with two crisp shirmals. As she handed them to him, her soft fingers brushed against his coarse, callused hand.

Gulam broke off a piece of the bread and fed the dog. 'I'm going to close the shop now,' she said. 'Do you need anything else?'

'I'll help pull the shutters down,' Gulam offered.

They locked the shop together and went up the staircase into Misreh's house where after talking for a few minutes, all the while staring at her, drunk with desire, he gently removed her pheran. She clutched his hand, gliding it under her frock, leading it above her belly button into the gap between her big soft breasts. As he fondled her, her lips parted, her breath growing uneven.

The hand slid lower down, down to the drawstring, where it yanked at a complicated knot.

They lay together naked on the hay-mat. A sodden stench rising from their twining bodies filled the room.

'I am a watul,' he said, entering her.

'*Mukur* watul,' she replied, biting his neck. Dirty cobbler.

'*Watul.*'

'*Mukur watul.*'

'*Watul, watul, watul.*'

'*Mukur watul, mukur watul, mukur watul.*'

When they were done, Gulam closed his eyes and snuggled up against her. But before he could fall asleep, she nudged him.

'I don't want you to go, but before the sermon ends you must.'

'Because your son will be returning home?'

'Yes. I'll meet you in the willow coppice by the river tonight.' She kissed him on the forehead. He gathered his clothes hurriedly and found the dog waiting for him patiently on the top step. He patted its head and went down the steps.

His house was sandwiched between two big buildings, three-storeyed structures with whitewashed walls and framed windows of pinewood, both owned by Rafiq Galwan. He crossed the road and went near the worktable he had placed under the staircase; he peered closely at the new gnawings by the woodworms in the wood. Inside the table were his sole possessions: anvil, hammer, nails, rubber soles, stitching thread, Fevicol, boxes of brown polish and black polish, and a bottle of white cream. He could see himself, an unkempt, ugly man, slightly built, haggard, miserable and exhausted. His head throbbed with weird thoughts; he heard bats flitting through the cramped dark of his room, and a herd of lambs bleating on the highway.

Jamshid's extraordinary voice resonated from the mosque. Gulam trudged upstairs and slammed the door shut behind him. He shut the windows, and securely latched them from inside. He sat down in the corner of the room, squeezed his eyes shut and jammed his fingers into his ears to ward off Jamshid's chanting. He felt utterly wretched, bitter and vengeful.

ॐ

The next morning, Gulam went downstairs to find 'Pasture' under the staircase. With an expression of deep remorse 'Pasture' handed him a basket of fruits, 'These are for you,' he said ruefully. 'The Syeds are happy with Jamshid.'

Gulam held the flat wicker basket covered with translucent amber paper, beneath which were triangles of pistachios, almonds, raisins, apricots and cashew nuts.

'Go feed this to Jamshid,' he said, pushing the peace offering away. 'I don't need any crap from him or his Syeds.'

As 'Pasture' turned to leave, Gulam grabbed the hammer from his table.

'If you ever came back here, I'll drive a nail into your head!' Gulam plumped down on his seat as 'Pasture' vanished through the doorway. He put the hammer down on the worktable and began to work.

A few minutes later, a jeep chugged into the street and halted in front of Gulam's door. The soldiers, standing erect on the seats, jumped down.

Major S balanced a gun in his hand. The gun was not a donkey's dick to caress and flaunt, but very much a weapon used to kill.

'Where's Jamshid?' he barked at Gulam.

'Sir,' Gulam said, rising from his seat, 'he did not come home last night.'

'Where is he, Jamshid, your son?' Major S repeated.

'Sir, he didn't come home last night. You can check my house.'

Major S nodded and Sunil and Raman thudded up the stairs.

'Give me your ID and sit down,' said Major S.

Gulam pulled out the card from his breast pocket and sat down.

Major S scrutinized the card carefully and Gulam stood up apprehensively.

'Sit down,' Major S snapped.

Gulam sat down only to bounce up again when he heard Sunil and Raman trooping down the staircase heavily.

'Major, there's no one upstairs,' Sunil reported.

Major S smiled unpleasantly at Gulam. He returned the ID card. 'Tell Jamshid to come to the camp tomorrow, early in the morning.'

'If he comes home, I will, sir,' Gulam replied.

Major S turned to leave when he espied a box of shoe polish on the worktable. He picked it up and sniffed it.

'Robin Polish,' he murmured.

'Yes, sir,' Gulam nodded. 'Robin Polish.'

'Is this high quality?' Major S asked.

'The highest quality of polish, sir,' Gulam replied.

Major S sucked at his front teeth, making a hissing sound. The two bodyguards who flanked him, gazed straight ahead.

Major S examined the rim of the box closely, his tongue sticking out with intense concentration.

'Open the lid,' he commanded.

Gulam's hands shook as he tried in vain to pry open the lid.

'Open … the … lid,' Major S repeated softly through clenched teeth.

Gulam's hands trembled even more.

'MADERCHOD, OPEN THE LID,' Major S bellowed. 'Your son is a close friend of Showkat.'

Gulam wept, his palms together in entreaty. 'Forgive me and my son, sir. Please spare us,' he pleaded.

'Grab his arms behind his back,' ordered Major S.

Sunil and Raman wrenched Gulam's arms behind him. Gulam kicked out in pain and Raman slapped his face. Major S opened the lid and dipped his fingertips into the shoe polish. He smeared this on Gulam's face while his henchmen held the hapless cobbler immobile.

12
The Boss's Account

~~~

Two months after the massacre, I returned to the spot. I stood at the edge of the highway, contemplating the tarmac moist with dew. If the tarmac could speak, it would tell me how it had felt when the bullets ripped through it. The darkness was about to vanish. I felt lonely thinking about the bodies felled here. In the middle of the road, I imagined a tree and the shadows of its severed branches floating through the dawn.

I lit a Revolution and looked east, across the highway. The sun would rise soon over the lovely brick houses of Bijbyor with their conical roofs and white windows and light up the drooping willow branches. No vehicles passed at that hour. The wisps of smoke suspended above my head, lingering above the tarmac, were like mute impressions of the last screams of the dead. I threw the Revolution with its burning tip onto the highway and walked into the street behind me. The shops were still shuttered, and the birds barely awake and numb in the nests. I listened to the sound of my own haunted footfalls, a feeble trot through the desolate dawn.

At the end of the street, I saw the river, subdued and glimmering. I asked the boatman, squatting at the stern, to take me to Kanelwan immediately. He was a middle-aged man with chiselled features set in dark, luminescent skin, and sported a stubble. However, both his ears were missing. Those missing ears! What a violation! What a pity!

I had met him once the last time I had visited this little town some thirty miles south of Srinagar, and I still thought of him as a stranger. But he glanced at me as if he could peer inside me directly and decipher all my intentions. I felt uncomfortable. I asked him his name, pretending I had forgotten it.

'You want to go to Shafiq Galwan's house because Showkat is there,' he said instead, moving his head up and down. 'Isn't that who you are looking for?' he asked.

I assented angrily and he lifted the oar from the bottom of the boat. Its tip was wet, covered with a film of water; he had ferried other people during the night.

'Hop on,' he said. As I sat myself down on the plank spanning the other end of his narrow dinghy, he pushed the tip of the oar against the bank of the falling muddy slope where the grass was sparse like the beard on the slope of his jaw. He sliced the water at angles, throwing a splash of needling sparks over the surface of the river.

'You'll see willows and more willows,' he announced. 'The pasture is vast and the paths are choked. Don't get lost in the willows, don't get bitten.'

The boat gliding above the deep waters was becoming heavy as though with the weight of the words streaming out of his mouth.

'You will see a mosque,' he said, striking the water again and jolting the boat, 'if you look in the right direction in the west. You'll see houses and men and women and children. You have ears all right. You'll hear their cries and you'll cry.'

His tone became direct and disruptive. I raised my head an inch and scoffed at him.

'Once you find the mosque,' he went on eloquently, 'even a blind man cannot miss Shafiq Galwan's house. It is right there, by the side of the mosque.'

I fished out a crumpled ten-rupee note from my pocket and threw it in his direction. He watched it fall like a brittle feather on the bottom of the boat. I resented him and didn't ask for change. He could have it all, good riddance, I thought. I stood up and scrambled out on to the bank. I ran away from this earless monster, not looking back once. I ran towards the west, following his instructions all the same. He was right; I saw the glinting bronze spire of the mosque through a tangle of twigs.

Showkat reclined on a cot in the middle of the courtyard. He was wholly intact, in a clean white shalwar and kameez made of gauzy cotton. People from Kanelwan and the town of Bijbyor had gathered around him in concentric circles; the adults standing in the outer rings and children in the inner section. I shouldered my way through the crowd. The sun that had climbed above the pasture sent down unimpeded streams of light. Showkat's face shone so radiantly that for one blinding moment I couldn't believe that this was the visage of a dead man. He still had the glistening and moist brown skin, the skin that had not dehydrated yet. On his lips rested a smile, vague but unvanquished. His eyelids were swollen and whoever had closed them – it could not have been Dilbar and, in all probability, it was Farhad, I came to reckon later – had not done a good job. There was a narrow gap between the lids through which I glimpsed the dark, soulless eyeballs. There was something utterly terrifying and abysmal about those blank, half-shut eyes of a freshly murdered man where life lay extinguished.

The men debated the loyalty of Showkat endlessly. Was he a renegade or a martyr? Was he a rebel or a collaborator? In their unceasing murmur of suspicion, I heard the women's wails coming from inside the house. Those cries were half-hearted and desperate. They floated above the courtyard and died as soon as they entered the dense pasture.

On the windows, thronged with young girls, I saw such beautiful eyes, bright gleaming eyes, sad clear eyes, eyes filled with innocence and purity of wonder, all looking at Showkat. I reached for and lifted his hand to my lips.

'Wake up,' I said. 'Wake up.'

Showkat did not wake up. He was always a reluctant riser in the mornings and loved to lie abed until he was forcibly yanked out of the duvets. It reminded me of the time when I was in Srinagar. He had arrived unannounced late one night at my lodge. I had happily invited him in. I allowed him to sleep in my bed, while I slept on the sofa in the living room.

One of those mornings, while he was still asleep, I went into the bedroom to rummage around in my chest of drawers for some of my stuff when I saw Sunil through the window that opened up to the street outside. Sunil was on short leave from the camp in Bijbyor and stayed in the apartment next to mine. He was in civil clothes. He hailed me in a friendly way.

'Who is this person asleep in your bed?' he asked, his eyes twinkling mischievously.

A guest, I smiled back. A very special guest and friend.

'I'll come over later,' Sunil said, raising his bag of breakfast: bananas, a bottle of milk and a box of Kellogg's cereal. 'Diya is waiting.'

I nodded and Showkat opened his eyes. Although Sunil was gone in a moment, his shadow, which the morning sun had cast on Showkat's face, seemed to linger on.

'If only he knew that you were the rebel ...' I said to Showkat and we chuckled.

I gave him my hand and hauled him out of bed. It was the first time in my life that I had made breakfast for someone. I scrambled eggs with onions and bell pepper. As soon as he had taken a shower, we breakfasted heartily and washed it all down with tea.

An hour later, Sunil arrived to play chess. He was great at manoeuvring his rooks and knights. Across the chessboard was Showkat, whose enthusiasm more than made up for his lack of experience and he put up a spunky fight. He advanced his pawns, although I suspected that he knew they were going to perish one by one. He played with a certain fearlessness and was resilient in his moves against Sunil's cold calculations.

Showkat had stowed his Kalashnikov beneath the bed and while the two went on playing in the sitting room, I worried about the fate of Diya and Pooja with whom I was well-acquainted by now, if Showkat went ahead with his plan to kill Sunil.

At night, I heard their laughter as Sunil became a pony for his little daughter, Diya, to ride on. I heard his lullabies to the four-year-old girl. Every day after coming back from the *Informer* offices, reporting incident after incident of crossfire and killings, the sound of the child's giggles raised my spirits.

Sunil rampaged destructively through Showkat's array of pawns, positioning his rooks and bishops around his king and blockading any chances of escape. Showkat shot me an angry glance and I shrugged non-commitally.

After Sunil left, Showkat asked, 'What should I do?'

I could not bear the idea of young Diya living the rest of her life without a father and I did my best to discourage his plan to annihilate Sunil.

'You cannot do it while you live under my roof,' I said. In a kamikaze strike, Showkat had destroyed Sunil's queen and bishop before his king had been struck down by a rook. He was clearly disappointed in me and left that evening.

ৎ

The first time I had visited the village, I had pondered the pasture. I had noticed that it was not like the pastures I caught a glimpse of in the English movies Safir kept watching on his laptop, the pastures drifting past the windows of the trains going out of London into the countryside. It did not have thick layers of fertile settled soil, though enough grass grew on it during the summer for all the cows of the village to graze. It was basically a bed of dry rocks and sand. The very thin layer of moist silted earth that was expediently deposited on the rocks in early spring by the river would be eroded when the rains grew profuse in autumn and the river flooded again. The willow trees that had obstructed my view of the river had separate trunks, but their branches were tangled together. I had walked into the middle of the pasture and had touched a willow. Its trunk was thick and the bark was hard and impenetrable. I could not picture the trunk individually; I could not think of it as something that belonged exclusively to the willow tree. It remained a part of the pasture, of the larger continuity, beyond and outside of me.

I remembered how huge Shafiq Galwan had appeared to me at our first meeting. He was six feet tall, with wide dimensions. He was a warm fellow who worked with his three younger brothers in the farms behind the village. He raised cattle, sheep and goats. The purest moments of joy for him were scattered through the evenings when from the farms he transported home ripe bales of crop, mustard in early summer and paddies in late autumn, on the backs of his horses. He barely bore any traces of the miserliness and guile of his harsh father who had been a young man when the famine had struck soon after the transfer of land to the peasants in 1953 by Sheikh Abdullah. Unlike his father, Shafiq Galwan had not starved in his adolescence, eating raw apricots and fried chickpeas to get by. He did not suffer from the anxiety of needing to feed a huge starving family that he had inherited. Following the creation of genetically modified seeds, the effects of the green revolution had been felt in Kashmir too. During his youth, the indigenous low-yielding variety of paddy, Mushkibudij, had been replaced with Budij China. The massive increase in the production had planted feelings of generosity and philanthropy in him, turning him into an easy lender of money and labour to the villagers. He was overflowing with gratitude. He vaguely guessed that it was a result of divine intervention that the production had increased massively; he did not realize that somewhere an inquisitive mind had toiled hard to question and mutate what was given us by God.

While these thoughts were taking shape in my mind, the image of the boatman's face recurred. I marvelled about the creator who, in the first place, had conceived of the boatman's face in his intelligence, and afterwards, like a supreme aesthete, had cast it in flesh and bones. I was distracted and I could not arrange my thoughts about Shafiq into a coherent whole because my mind veered towards the violence of the human hands that had cut off the ears and mutilated the boatman's beauty.

I stared hard at Shafiq Galwan, trying to concentrate. Unlike him, it dawned on me, God had never had any rational appeal for me. The appeal, when it was there, was purely aesthetic. It was odd and petty to be jealous of Shafiq. He was firmly moored to his place; of his own setting he was a natural emanation. Despite his increasing prosperity and Kashmir's sudden descent into turmoil, not once did he even dream of abandoning his home, family or Kanelwan. I was aware of his presence that I shared with him, with his pair of eyes, the view. He mitigated the terror of isolation and estrangement that the pasture unfailingly stirred in me. He enhanced me; and in diminishing my fear, he diminished me.

I rose through the ranks, from an ordinary reporter and through many levels of correspondence to become the bureau chief of the *Informer*. During these two decades, I witnessed the worst. However, this ascent in my career necessitated befriending officials and authorities who committed the atrocities and squeezing bits of information from them. It was necessary to be shrewd and alert. To establish my supremacy in the hierarchy, I threw my weight around, belittling my colleagues. I ensured that I conveyed to them where they stood beneath me. And then, with a radical shift in the other direction, I said good and kind words to appease and create an impression of empathy.

With each rung that I climbed, with each story I found and broke to reach the top of the ladder, something in me, like a handful of fertile moist soil deposited on my being, withered and fell off. The appeal of a just god dwindled until it vanished altogether. I was left hollow and purposeless. I became solitary and conscious of my solitude. I frequented

Café Barbarica every night and drank myself into a stupor. I wanted to cut off all my ties with the people of power in Srinagar; I wanted to be a complete vagrant. The desire to retreat kept mounting until it became oppressive. The only way to drown it was by drinking more and more.

In the mornings, I woke up with a hangover and a sharp headache. I wished I could escape to some remote place, away from Srinagar, where the city's brutal soldiers and conniving policemen and scarred civilians could not reach me.

During the day at the *Informer*, I was loud and unproductive; I barked at my subordinates as I failed to dispense my duties.

At night when I returned to my lodge, Safir told me about his fantasies of travel roused by the movies he watched. I pictured him, and in those moments I bitterly envied him, as he pictured himself, seated comfortably by the glass window rolling past a pasture. However, before his arrival in a remote English village, I fancied that the train was hit by an explosion, putting an end to his fanciful escapades.

ॐ

'In the pasture,' Shafiq Galwan said, 'there is a small house. It was there that Showkat cut Major S's right arm.'

I listened to him, without taking notes.

Major S had entered that hovel where Showkat, hanging upside down from the ceiling, lay in wait with a dagger. He had descended with speed and slammed the door shut on Sunil before he could follow the major inside. Showkat grabbed Major S's arm and his dagger ripped through his uniform, sinking deep into the startled man's inner elbow. Recovering from the shock, Major S kicked his assailant hard in the chest, shoving him against the wall. Major S ran out of the house, but his arm came loose and he left it behind. Sunil charged in, pounced on Showkat and snatched his bloodied dagger. He handcuffed and blindfolded him and led him away into the army's garrison.

Shafiq Galwan told me that he didn't know whose command they followed after this because Major S was sent off to the army hospital in Srinagar. But when Major S returned to the camp, he told Sunil to release Showkat immediately. The villagers were amazed that the soldiers did not imprison Showkat, neither did they beat him or shoot him dead.

Shafiq Galwan found Showkat in the same shack where he was captured. He was wearing a clean kameez and shalwar. He was in a deep sleep on a spotless white sheet in the corridor. Shafiq woke him up by shaking his shoulder. Showkat couldn't recognize him but begged him to bring him some food. Shafiq ran back through the pasture, came home and asked his wife to warm up the chicken and rice that she had made the previous night.

When Shafiq went back, he found Dilbar and Farhad standing at Showkat's head, their faces masked with black scarves. Both had placed their Kalashnikovs on the floor beside Showkat. He lay with his eyes half-open, the veins on his forehead distended and blue.

Shafiq immediately understood what had happened and dropped to his knees by Showkat's feet. The box of food fell out of his nerveless fingers. He glanced at Dilbar and wondered how Showkat must have shook and writhed his legs; how he must have struggled when one of them or both – who knew – grabbed his neck and squeezed his throat so hard that they blocked the flow of air and blood. His whole body must have convulsed as his pounding heart stopped beating altogether.

'Who did this?' Shafiq had asked.

'I strangled him,' Dilbar replied, removing his mask.

Shafiq had grabbed his collar. Was he not your own? he had screamed.

But Dilbar shoved him away. 'How could he come back in one piece from the camp then? How come he is wearing the best shalwar and kameez that he ever wore in his life? It wasn't like he had gone to visit his in-laws that he should come back dressed in finery. Had he?'

ॐ

The sun slanted above the roof of the house behind us. The courtyard filled with wails. I walked away into the pasture where a faint wind had begun to blow from the direction of the river. Behind me, Shafiq Galwan kept calling my name. He wanted me to stay for the wake and eat the meal brought over by the neighbours. Showkat was like one of Shafiq Galwan's own kinsmen. I did not stop. Although my stomach was empty, I was not hungry. I always considered funeral food as inauspicious and it nauseated me, evoking the smell of the dead. The sight of the chicken dishes and kebabs that the neighbours had cooked killed my appetite. The festive fare, intended to facilitate forgetting, had a reverse impact on me.

I walked on until a fear seized me and I started running. I ran towards the river and a pack of stray dogs followed me. I speeded up, ducking under the tangles, and the dogs gave chase barking enthusiastically, their mouths agape.

I was as breathless as the dog, the one with a dark snout that had managed to reach me. I'm fairly sure that the dogs would have slain me that day and I would have become fodder for the pasture had the boatman not advanced with his oar and struck at the head of the dog. Reeling from the unexpected blow, the dog fell to the ground, its furious growl turning into a sad whine. The other dogs took fright and stopped their headlong rush towards me. They growled and dug their forepaws into the sand before slowly backing away from their new adversary armed with an oar.

I was silent. I was expecting a told-you-so from him. But he held his peace. With concentration, he struck the water rhythmically, now a darker shade of green in the evening that had descended on the river. He deftly steered the boat against the current, cutting through the wind.

I saw the spot, the darkening mouth of the street, where he had picked me up that morning, and I asked him about his missing earlobes.

'Before I tell you how my ears were cut off, I want to share with you an old story in my family.'

I was grateful to him; I listened with patience.

'I know you, you know,' he remarked.

How did he know me?

'I once visited my brother in Srinagar. He ferries under Zero Bridge. It was there that I saw you, going in and out of the big building on the bank that I suppose is your office. I was staying with him in the boathouse right outside on the Jhelum and when in the evenings, he was tired, I took over from him which was when I ferried you. You probably thought I was him.'

I apologized.

'It's okay. We kind of look alike.'

I smiled.

'You're a journalist.' He frowned. 'As soon as you write a few stories, you get cocky like the policemen. If you had only paid some attention as you strolled along the bank smoking those long cigarettes that are so fashionable these days – what are they called? Yes, Revolution. Ah, I love their scent!'

I took out my packet of Revolution and gave it to him.

'Do you have a matchbox?'

I rose and extracted the box of matches from my trouser pocket. I asked him to slow down the boat. I stepped closer and lit the cigarette.

'Love this fragrance,' he said, taking a deep, appreciative drag.

I told him I was glad and smiled.

He noticed me looking closely at the blank spaces where his ears ought to have been. Taking another long drag, he indicated his right lobe.

'As for this,' he said, tapping the missing organ, exhaling smoke, 'my ancestors were from Srinagar. One day, many centuries ago, one of my forefathers happened to be at a funeral. They were walking on what is now called Zero Bridge, just as the Afghans rode into the city for the first time. They collided with the procession. The Afghan leading the cavalcade stopped the procession by pointing his lance at the pallbearers. He asked them to lower the corpse to the ground. Then he grabbed my forefather and smiled malevolently at him. He leaned towards his face, as though he was going to whisper something sweet in his ear. With a savage violence, the Afghan bit off my ancestor's earlobe and spat it out. When one of his tribesmen asked him why he had done that, he replied that as soon as the dead man was interred in the earth, he would convey the news to the kingdom of the dead that the Afghans had arrived in Kashmir.'

The boatman stopped and handed me the smouldering cigarette. He pulled the oar out of the water. 'Those fucking Afghans,' he said, casting the oar into the boat. He leaned over, scooped up some water and splashed it on the orifice.

'I still feel a strange tingling here as though recounting how my forefather lost his ear has resurrected the horror that my ancestor lived through and I can feel the Afghan's teeth right now.'

He picked up his oar angrily and began to row the boat that had drifted down with the current.

'I lost my ears a few months ago. Do you know who cut off my ears with a knife? You came to visit when there was a lot of gunfire on the bridge after the Friday prayer at the mosque and fifty-one worshippers were killed on the highway. On day that you came to interview me, Sunil took me to the camp with him in the evening. Major S interrogated me about Showkat and his friends and whether it was I who had ferried them across the river.

'I did not confirm this, but because in fact I had, Sunil grabbed my right ear and dragged me to a room where a cauldron of water simmered with an electric immersion heater placed on its rim. Sunil grabbed my hair and threatened to plunge my head into the water if I did not tell him the truth. So, I confessed.'

I passed the cigarette back to him, its tip momentarily brightening in the heaving dark.

'When he brought me out to the veranda, Major S was sitting there having a snack. He smiled as Sunil nodded at him and cordially asked me to sit in the chair beside him. He summoned his cook and told him to give me a cup of tea. I was terrified but he seemed genuinely friendly. Suddenly, before the tea arrived, he turned and grabbed my neck and shoved my face on to the patio table by the bowl of snacks. I don't quite remember how I felt in that moment. He whipped out a knife with tremendous speed and sliced it across my ears.

'He kicked me from behind and I fell to the ground, squirming in agony, my hands covering the bleeding sides of my head. Major S folded the penknife with a snap and put it back into his pocket. He calmly pushed the bloodied potato chips aside and fished out a clean sliver from the bowl and ate it.'

We had reached the bank by now. The tip of his Revolution was still smouldering. The boatman took one more drag. I put my hand inside my pocket, but he shook his head.

'I do not need the fare, not always,' he said and smiled.

13
The Night of Broken Glass

—❦—

Fatima sat by a wall-sized window, scribbling. Her notebooks were scattered about her on the fur carpet. Ample light streamed in through the glass pane. The white ceiling fan hung lifeless without electricity; the air inside the sitting room was stuffy and static.

Fatima glanced sideways and noticed me by the door. She jumped up and ran to me, throwing her sweaty little arms around my neck. Her hot cheeks brushed against my stubble. Her eyes lit up as she covered my face with kisses. 'Uncle, let's go,' she cried excitedly.

We entered a dense clump of willows through a cluster of brown brick houses. The canopy formed by the profusion of branches and leaves was lit from above by the sun in descent and stretched all the way to the riverbank where the sky came into view again, vast and wide. Fatima led me down to the flat polished bed of rocks jutting out of the bank. She thrust her hands forward to shoo away a fish and I held her to make sure she didn't fall headlong into the river.

I was Fatima's age, six, when her mother, Nuzhat, disappeared from home for four days. On the fifth day, when she returned home, she slunk out of the house in the evening, crossed the grove and sped to the river and jumped in.

Showkat was alive then and so was Mother. It was he who pulled Nuzhat out of the deep waters and flung her on the bank at Mother's feet. Mother, almost insane with worry, had thrown off her headgear and was tearing out her hair in desperation.

Later that night, when I crept into Nuzhat's room, she was under clean, white bedcovers, her head propped up on a soft pillow. She had almost drowned; her lungs had filled with water. Her face was pale. Her eyes, criss-crossed with a web of fine red veins, were filled with a strange sadness.

'Killing yourself won't bring Rosy back,' Mother said, brushing aside a lock of Nuzhat's hair from her forehead.

'Rosy's body was bloated beyond recognition, Mother. I'm not even sure that it was her at all,' Nuzhat replied and drew the sheet over her face.

Although Mother, Showkat and I did our best to speak to her, Nuzhat insisted that we leave her alone. She fell asleep without touching the bowl of mutton stew that Mother had made for her.

As we went into the kitchen, Showkat said: 'I'll have to leave, Mother, before Major S comes here.'

'Have food and go,' Mother urged. But Showkat shook his head and got ready to leave.

I followed him into the corridor. 'What happened to Rosy?' I asked.

He ignored me and went on tying the laces of his shoes, without raising his head. Then he straightened up and said, 'Something so terrible that only jumping into the river could drown.'

༄

Fatima wrenched herself free and kicked off her flip-flops. She climbed on to the bank and ran along it, her cream cotton dress, hemmed with miniature gardenias, billowing out in the cool air. She muttered fragments of rhymes, creating her own rhyme:

Johnny Johnny, yes Papa
Jack and Jill, no Papa.

I held her flip-flops in my lap and Fatima curled up against me. I passed to her the pebble I had picked up from the grass. She flung it into the river and the pebble plopped down, creating concentric ripples on the water's surface. The sun sank into the horizon behind us and a flock of cranes flew across the sky. Amused and startled, Fatima pointed a chubby finger at the magnificent birds. 'Shin Chan, Ninja Hathode, Ninja, Ninja …' she shouted.

We walked upstream. The bank curved and climbed. The grass was thicker here and drenched in dew. Across the darkening willow spinney, the sky was an indigo blue, saw-toothed by the silhouettes of the roofs angling upward. As the twilight faded, the stars began to appear.

Fatima clutched a tuft of grass. The dewdrops slid off the blades into her palm and slipped through her fingers, splattering her dress. I combed my fingers through her dark tresses and Fatima grew calm.

The next morning, Fatima woke up late and missed her school bus. Nuzhat rebuked her sharply when she entered the kitchen. Fatima climbed up the steep staircase to my study on the second storey and pushed open the heavy door. There, behind a pile of books on the floor, surmounted by a fresh copy of *The Night of Broken Glass*, she found me asleep on my bed.

'Uncle, the bus has left. What do I do now?' she asked, tugging at my shirt impatiently.

I opened my eyes. Her eyes were large, black-lashed and moist. Her face, a lot like my own, had dirty smudges.

'Uncle,' she repeated plaintively, 'I missed the bus. Will you take me to school in the local bus?'

I nodded. I walked her to the basin in the corridor and washed her face. I dabbed it delicately with my soft, white towel until it was clean and dry.

It was a bright April morning. I carried her on my shoulder and we walked along the verge of the dusty road strewn with bright shingles. The street meandered out of the village and through an apricot grove in pink, incipient bloom to Mir Bazar. The village grocery market was built around the intersection where the narrow road from the village intersected the broad highway. The sun seethed overhead, burning the black tarmac. The dust seemed to be set ablaze over the rusting shutters.

I gently lowered her down from her lofty perch and we stood at the curb in front of Gulam, who was hunched over his worktable. When I turned to greet him, I noticed that his back was bent, and his head dangled from the long, thin stalk of his neck. He was a hairy, unkempt person with a coarse and wrinkled face; he had the wizened expression of a man who was prematurely decaying. He held the wooden handle of the hammer in his hand, its iron head on the anvil.

Fatima was in her uniform, a blue silk frock, black stockings and shoes. Undaunted by the heat, she smiled. She held her small lunch-box in her hands while I carried her heavy schoolbag.

'Uncle, that soldier doesn't look like us,' Fatima remarked, looking across the highway.

'He doesn't belong here,' I replied.

'What is he doing here?'

'He is trying to catch Ninja Hathode.'

'Did he catch Ninja?'

I raised my eyebrow, not knowing how to respond. She frowned, closely scrutinizing the grim-faced soldier. She hugged her little lunch-box.

'Poor thing. Why doesn't he go home? Doesn't he miss his Mama?' she asked.

'He goes home when he is on vacation. When he misses his Mama, he plays with Ninja.'

Fatima smiled at him. The soldier crossed the road to the cobbler. In the mirage of heat rising from the tarmac, his shoulders sagged under the weight of his Kalashnikov and the grenades in his two bulging breast pouches.

As he moved towards Fatima, Gulam tightened his grip on the handle, hammering down on the anvil.

Fatima extended her hand to the soldier, but he walked past her and stopped in front of me. At close range, his grimness was more pronounced, with hues of tattered apathy.

I stepped past the soldier, towing Fatima along. When the soldier walked away, Gulam stopped pounding the anvil.

ॐ

After I dropped Fatima at school in Khanbal, I stood hot and crammed in the aisle of an overcrowded bus. It was time for the convoy to leave the cantonment and the bus had halted near the gates. Through the glass pane, I saw a tall, erect, concrete wall, covered in a tangled mesh of dark-green wire. The army vehicles passed by close to the bus, filling its interior with their groaning and acrid fumes.

When I reached Mir Bazar, I saw Gulam again. He sat behind his crumbling worktable, his head hanging in reticence and depression. I walked up to him and held his arm. He pushed my hand away irritably.

'Please tell me what happened to Rosy,' I whispered.

He darted a malevolent glance at me and turned away, shaking his head. Then he walked up the staircase into the small room that served as his home.

I followed him in. The room smelt of dust, rats and shoe polish. The windows were shut and the room was dark. He had driven dozens of nails into the brick walls from which a variety of shoes were suspended. He sat down on the cot in the corner of the room without inviting me to sit as well. I could still see him, so I did not ask him to open the window. I instinctively knew that the beams of light would snatch something precious from him and shatter his fragile, private world. In the course of our conversation, he revealed that that something was a memory from his past that over the years he had clung to fiercely. Paradoxically, the need to preserve the memory emerged from his necessity to shield himself from it.

'Look around,' he said. This was all that remained of that fateful night. That pair he pointed to over there, those soft brown loafers, they were his son's shoes, yes, they belonged to Jamshid. That one black loafer, that was Syed Anzar Shah's. Those yellow shoes with hard soles and square heals, they shod Nadim's humongous feet. He had collected them outside the camp where he had searched in vain for Jamshid's dead body. Although most of the other bodies were found and buried, only Jamshid's body was not found on the highway outside the camp. Even the blood had been washed away by the rain that fell that afternoon soon after the Friday prayers, and all that remained were the shoes, abandoned and scattered. He did not see even a single corpse then, not one out of fifty-six.

He had visited Misreh at noon. She was caressing his hair when they heard the gunshots and stampeding crowds. He wanted to go out and see what the matter was but Misreh held him back, saying it was not safe. She latched the door to her house from inside and they sat quietly until it became quiet and the downpour started. He was filled with a dark fear because across the road, the entire town of Bijbyor had begun to wail. When the rainfall grew torrential it drowned out the sounds of the laments.

When he eventually tore himself away from Misreh and came out, a hush had fallen on the highway. The smell of blood was supplanted by the smell of the earth awash with the rain. He walked towards the mosque. How did he know that his son was dead and that he was looking for Jamshid's body? It was not a mere premonition or a wish he had buried over the years after his alienation from his son. He had deduced it from the manner in which Major S had told him to send Jamshid to the military camp. Looking into Major S's eyes at the time, he had seen vengeance and sensed danger. He had felt a pang of joy at the possibility of his son's murder; the son whose presence diminished him and, at the same time, filled him with pride.

On the highway, outside the camp and the bridge where the bodies had fallen, he desperately searched for his son's body. He knew he would no longer have to bear Jamshid's eloquent voice or his extraordinarily luminous face. That night – and every night after that – when he returned to the cramped darkness of his room he confronted the fact of Jamshid's demise. Peering into the dark cavern of death's mouth as it swallowed his head, leaving his neck stuck between its jagged, white fangs, he became fearless. He forgot that he was a watul and became oblivious to the distinction between the Syeds and the Sheikhs. 'It's ridiculous,' he shouted out loud. He wanted to find Syed Anzar Shah's body and Syed Aslam Shah's body, because he wanted to give them a decent funeral. He wanted to mourn for Nadim and call him by his beautiful name, *Nadimo, Nadimo, Nadimo*, the way his mother called him, even though Nadim had been mean to Gulam. Heckler though he was and Misreh's only child, Gulam never wanted to call him by the demeaning nickname of 'Pasture'. But now all of them, all the boys and men whose shoes he had polished, were gone. What was left were the shoes. As long as Gulam lived, he would guard them and polish them religiously.

Outside, as night fell, the road emptied of vehicles, the shops closed and the market became mute. I could barely see Gulam. He had collapsed in the corner and the terrifying thought darted through my mind that perhaps he was dead as well.

I stood frozen for a while until I heard the sound of teeth grinding. I saw Gulam's silhouette sit up against the wall.

Fifteen years ago in 1993, he began in his rasping voice, on the evening of 28 April, Major S smeared shoe polish on his face. He went so far as to dip his fingertips into the box of polish and insert his fingers into Gulam's mouth. It was an act of pure misanthropy and sadism that defied comprehension and nearly drove Gulam insane. But Misreh, that kind woman, saved him again. She had seen him through the window of her house, seen how his mouth was desecrated. She cursed Major S as she hurried across the street to Gulam. She took him home and kept him with her until she left him five years later, succumbing to typhoid. He left Bijbyor that very day and went to Mir Bazar because he could not bear to live in the street where she no longer lived. He loved her because she had washed his mouth clean of the polish and had given him a tumbler of milk. When Nadim returned home that evening, she told him straightaway that Gulam was going to live with her and that he was as good as her husband and that she would no longer consider herself a widow. Her son was taken aback by this unexpected announcement. Nadim flung his mother's pots and pans on the kitchen floor and flounced out of the house in a dudgeon. Had she known that her son had so little time left in this world, Misreh would never have berated or cursed him that day. Nadim joined the protest outside the camp. Shafiq Galwan, a survivor from Kanelwan, had testified that when Jamshid led the crowd to the bridge, Nadim flung his body across Jamshid's, absorbing the first hail of bullets. He sacrificed his life for his friend.

Gulam never found Jamshid's body. When he arrived at the highway outside the camp that evening, it was still drizzling. The tarmac, clean of the blood, was covered with glass splinters. He assumed that the soldiers had stopped some passenger trucks and broken their windshields and rear-view mirrors. But somehow it seemed that this was something more than just that. He looked around, at the mosque across the lawn. All fifteen windows in the front had been smashed. He went into the mosque. It was gloomy and dark inside.

He stepped over the piles of broken glass and made his way towards the huge wooden minaret in the middle. This was the first time that he had been inside the mosque when it was completely empty. He was frightened. The windows, the light fixtures including the massive chandelier and even the stoppered vials of rosewater were all smashed to smithereens. He remembered the hypnotic eloquence and grandeur of Jamshid's voice. In the spectacle of destruction around him, the abandonment and silence became intolerable. A wave of sorrow coursed through him. He faced Mecca and begged Allah for strength. He lowered his head and wept, giving the summons for prayer.

He walked past the veranda of the mosque through the long lawns to the edge of the highway. The slivers of glass pierced the sides of his feet that weren't protected by his footwear, making them bleed. Imagine the force of the blows delivered to the windows from inside that had sent the shards flying across through the night. He crept into the camp, but the mansion was deserted now. The soldiers, fearing an attack from the natives, had left. He went to the bridge and stood in the middle and saw nothing but the whimpering, wet dog limping towards him.

Gulam knew that during an argument with his mother, Nadim had told her that Major S was building a huge casket out of the planks of the maple he had had felled within the camp.

When Gulam mentioned this, I wondered whether Major S, wanting to fill his masterpiece with the most perfect body in Kashmir, Jamshid's, had thrown the casket into the river in lieu of the burial for a young leader. But Gulam continued with his tale. He was perplexed at why only his son's body had disappeared completely, if the soldiers had fired at Misreh's and Anzar's sons as well.

Misreh told him later that Major S had gone directly to Shah Manzil after smearing his face with boot polish. The very next day, Gulam saw Nuzhat and the inhabitants of Bijbyor fishing Rosy's pale, waterlogged body out of the Jhelum. It barely looked like her. There were bruises all over the corpse.

Gulam was standing by a willow when he saw them bring the body up in a fisherman's net. And there she was, his beautiful daughter-in-law, the girl for whom Jamshid had given up his father. He was curious to see Rosy. When he saw the body blued as if she had been bludgeoned to death with a saucepan, he covered his eyes with his hands.

Major S had found Syed Anzar Shah relaxing in his garden. Every police officer who had been posted in Bijbyor had invariably dropped in to pay their respects to him, so, Anzar Shah had been expecting a visit from Major S for some time now. That evening when he saw Major S and two of his bodyguards, Raman and Sunil, advancing towards him, he stood up and held out his hand in a friendly manner. Major S shook it very briefly. He sat across the patio table from Syed Anzar Shah, the impeccable host, who offered to provide refreshments and cordially asked him what he would like to have.

'The president of the Jammu Kashmir Youth Front,' Major S replied.

'You would loathe him,' Anzar Shah said with a chuckle. 'He is too bright a kid.' Then turning around, he called for tea. Minutes later, Rosy emerged with the tea tray.

As she leaned over the table, Major S looked at her, measuringly.

Anzar Shah told Rosy to go away and dispensed the tea himself from the steel kettle into the white, porcelain cups. He wanted Jamshid, Major S stated baldly, taking a sip of the scalding brew. Syed Anzar Shah told him that Jamshid was not there in the house.

Major S reiterated that he wanted Jamshid and rose, pouring the tea over the grass lawn. Although Syed Anzar Shah was angry, he stayed silent. Sunil and Raman aimed their guns at Syed Anzar Shah's head.

'Where is he?' Major S repeated. Syed Anzar Shah remained obstinately mute. Major S grabbed his shirt collar and slapped him. Then he yanked at his beard and slapped him again. The white skullcap on Anzar Shah's head fell down, and Major S grabbed his hair and slapped him. 'Boys,' he said, 'gag him and beat him until he reveals where he has hidden Jamshid.'

Sunil sealed the old man's mouth with Sellotape. Raman kicked him in his stomach and his face.

Major S went into the kitchen and latched the door from inside. Rosy and Hasin rose in alarm, backing away from him. He seized Hasin by her hair and hurled her against the wall. She fell down, unconscious.

Major S grabbed Rosy, who was trying to wriggle out through the window. He cupped her cheeks with one rough hand. 'Jamshid's bride!' he jeered. 'He fucks you every night. You must know where he is.'

She lowered her eyes, shaking her head. 'Where is he?' he bellowed. She stared at him, wordlessly. He grabbed her hand, placed it on his crotch and rubbed himself. Then he unzipped his fly, his fingers still holding her hand. With his other hand, he opened fire at the utensils, breaking the porcelain plates and sending shards flying about the room.

'It happened in this sequence,' Gulam said. Misreh, who had entered Shah Manzil for the very first time in her life to mourn with Hasin, had told him all this. Hasin had recited the tragic story in an elegy as the people shrouded Rosy. When Hasin had regained consciousness in the kitchen, Major S was nibbling at her daughter's thighs.

I heard Gulam get to his feet. His entire body was trembling. I stepped nearer and hugged him. But he writhed in my embrace as though my touch irritated him and filled him with fresh spasms of internal pain. 'Let me go, let me go,' he protested.

I left him and made my way to the riverbank. A thin layer of clouds covered the sky. The light of the lanterns inside the houses was vague and dim. All I could think of now was Fatima. In my mind, her face was superimposed on Nuzhat's which was superimposed in turn on Rosy's. I shook my head hard to throw off this conjured image.

The lanterns in the windows were extinguished. I rose, groping blindly in the pitch dark. I stumbled into a willow and scraped my elbow. I walked home, nursing my bleeding elbow.

I wondered whether my encounter with Gulam was real, or if I had merely imagined his apparition and his voice.

As I pushed the entrance door open, Fatima darted out of the kitchen into the corridor. Betrayed. I had broken my promise to take her for a walk before nightfall. Her eyes were swollen. I leaned forward and enfolded her in my arms. She furiously shoved my head away, hitting my face with her little hands. One moment, she was defiant and angry. The next, she was holding my neck in her arms, melting me in her embrace.

Acknowledgments

❦

Writing this book has been a long, transformative journey. Without my family and my friends, I do not think I could have come so far.

I am grateful to my mother Hajira, my father, Ismaiel, my brothers Showkat and Ajaz, my sisters, Nusrat and Gulshan, Nargis Didi, Sumaya, Ajeh, and all the younger Rathers.

Basharat Peer for his unfailing faith, and Wajahat Ahmad for his compassion. Idris Hassan Bhat, Sohail Mir, Sajad Sheikh, Asgar Qadri, Yael Plitmann, Saiba Varma, Adil Bhat and Abid Rather for their wonderful friendship.

Gaiutra Bahadur for being a superb first reader, Mirza Waheed for his enthusiasm, and Siddhartha Deb for his wise words. Irfan Bukhari and Suviad Yasin for their companionship. Sameer Mohammad and Mohammad

Junaid and Melissa for opening the doors of their houses in New York to me.

Almost the entire book was written in Tallahassee, from the fall of 2015 to the summer of 2017. At Florida State University where I am pursuing a doctorate in Creative Writing, I am indebted to my teachers from whose workshops and seminars I benefitted immensely: Skip Horack, Robert Olen Butler, Elizabeth-Stuckey French, Bob Shacochis, Lisa Wakamiya, Diane Roberts, Anne Coldiron and John Mac Kilgore. I am also thankful to Professor Andrew Epstein for running such a fabulous programme.

Graduate school has its own challenges but my colleagues and friends kept me going. I can't name them all but the ones I must are Whitney Gilchrist, S.J. Sindhu, C.J. Houser, Misha Rai, Karen Tucker, Zack Strait, Iheoma Nwachukwu, Obioma Calvin Umeozor, Lee Paterson, Theodor, Mat, Munib, Clancy, Paige, Colleen, Jenny, Reema Barakat, Huma Sheikh, Amanda Furiasse and Sher Khan.

My gratitude is due to Zahid Rafiq who stood by me at a very depressing time in my life. I am also thankful to Muzamil Jaleel and Majid Maqbool for sharing with me their stories about Kashmir.

At HarperCollins India, I want to thank my editor, Rea Mukherjee. Her brilliance infused the text with a new life.

At Sangam House, I want to thank Arshia Sattar for giving me space to write what would become the Bijbyor stories placed towards the end of the book.

Finally, I want to thank Hera Naguib: *Your presence is a sacred music undulating beneath these lines.*